# CHRISTMAS
# WITH THE DUKE

# CHRISTMAS
# WITH THE DUKE

KATRINA CUDMORE

**MILLS & BOON**

First published in Great Britain 2018
by Mills & Boon, an imprint of HarperCollins*Publishers*
1 London Bridge Street, London, SE1 9GF

Large Print edition 2019

© 2018 Katrina Cudmore

ISBN: 978-0-263-08203-6

MIX
Paper from
responsible sources
FSC™ C007454

This book is produced from independently certified
FSC™ paper to ensure responsible forest management.
For more information visit www.harpercollins.co.uk/green.

Printed and bound in Great Britain
by CPI Group (UK) Ltd, Croydon, CR0 4YY

To Ava, my modern girl full of wit, intelligence, acceptance and ambition.

The world is yours to conquer.

# CHAPTER ONE

'GOOD GIRL, CIARA, just another foot to go and you'll be there.'

Despite her shaking legs, Ciara Harris could not help but grin to herself at her boss's good-natured encouragement. Sean was the head gardener at Loughmore Castle and, having known Ciara since she was a teenager, at times still treated her as one despite the fact that she was now thirty years of age.

Her smile soon faded, however, when she made the fatal mistake of looking down from her twenty-foot-high perch up on the stepladder. The Connemara marble floor of the Great Hall swam up and then back down in a sickening vortex.

She grasped the stepladder's metal rail for dear life and cast an unhappy eye over the reason she was twenty feet up in the air. The fine-boned angel, dressed in gold silk, her cheeks painted with a dash of pink blush, calmly considered

Ciara back, as though wondering why she was making such a fuss.

Standing with Sean at the base of the stepladder, looking way too amused for her own good, Libby the head chef at Loughmore called up to Ciara. 'Sometime in the next year would be helpful, Ciara. I've five layers of Christmas cake to ice and a ton of petit fours to make for tomorrow night's lighting ceremony,'

Ciara scowled down at Libby, who had one foot casually propped on the bottom rung of the ladder, with a glass of mulled wine in one hand and a mince pie in the other, and muttered through clenched teeth, 'I nominate *you* to climb up here next Christmas.'

'Oh, no, the pleasure will be all yours until a new member of staff is recruited,' Libby called back, with a tad too much relish.

Given the amused expressions of all thirty or so of the other Loughmore staff, who had come into the hall to watch the final finish to the tree decoration and, more to the point, rush to the buffet table, to partake in the refreshments Libby's team had organised, Ciara guessed they shared Libby's entertainment at Ciara's terror.

*'Gird your loins...'* That was what her granddad

had used to say to her as she'd buried herself beneath her blankets as a teenager, when he'd called her before dawn in order to polish the vast marble floor she was now suspended over. To this day she still had no idea what that expression really meant, but she knew it had been his way of telling her just to get on with it.

Ciara's mum was definitely cut from the same cloth as her grandad. As a child, whenever Ciara had grumbled about a playground slight or wished she had a sister to play with, or a dad who would come to watch her play football like all the other dads, her mum would say, 'Don't overthink things, Ciara. Accept that life is unfair, put a smile on your face and just get on with it.'

Which she now needed to do.

Tentatively she moved on to the next step, inhaling deeply of the pine-scented air, before humming a Christmas classic in the hope of channelling some of the festive spirit.

Every Christmas Sean cut down a Noble Fir from Loughmore Wood. It was always huge—it had to be to suit its new home, the Great Hall at Loughmore Castle, which lived up to its title by having a forty-foot vaulted timber ceiling. But this year Sean had surpassed himself by cutting down a stunning blue needle perfectly symmetrical twenty-four-foot specimen.

It had taken the gardening crew of five an entire day to transport it, install it and hang two thousand lights and the endless baubles the Benson family had collected over the years from the tree's branches.

Sean had rather cleverly waited until the last moment to announce that it was a castle tradition that the newest employee always had the honour of placing the delicate porcelain angel.

For a few moments Ciara had actually bought that story. But then she had spotted the mischief twinkling in Sean's eyes, and the elbowing amongst her fellow gardeners. Honour, indeed. More like the short straw. Obviously no one else wanted the task—especially when Libby's mince pies were on offer.

She had tried to protest that technically she *wasn't* the newest employee, given she had worked in Loughmore as a cleaner during her school summer holidays. But her protest had fallen on deaf ears in the buffet table raid.

Anyway, as the only female member of staff on the gardening team, and a conservation and heritage horticulturalist to boot, Ciara knew that, apart from Sean, the rest of the gardening team were sceptical about her role and her ideas.

Only yesterday there had been a stand-off between her and one of the others, who had wanted to cut some holly for decorating the castle. Ciara had tried to explain to him just how important the holly and its berries were for the birds and small animals, both as a source for food and shelter, but her colleague had shaken his head and muttered, 'You're pure cracked, Ciara…' before walking away.

So, ignoring the screaming alarm bells in her brain, she had grabbed hold of the angel and begun the climb. It was only when she'd been halfway up the stepladder that the voice of reason in her head had finally broken through her indignation at her co-workers and pointed out that she was terrified of heights.

But now, determined to continue on, aided by the combination of singing and her refusal to look down, she soon reached the top of the tree. Gingerly she leant into the branches, trying her best to ignore the pine needles stabbing against her bare forearms.

The ladder wobbled ever so slightly. Below her she heard a few gasps.

'Steady now…take it easy,' Sean called up.

Ciara leant in even further, keen to get the job over and done with. Inching forward, she managed to place the angel on the top branch, using her fingertips to straighten it when she slouched to the left.

Below her, applause rang out.

She'd done it!

Her elation lasted all of five seconds—until it dawned on her that she now had to climb back down.

Gripping the rails, she began her descent, her feet blindly searching for each tread beneath her.

The Christmas tree was positioned in front of the Great Hall's vast Pugin fireplace and a gold over-mantel mirror. A few steps down from the top, in a gap between the branches, Ciara grimaced when she caught her reflection in the mirror. Pine needles were scattered in her hair and a smear of dirt stained the collar of her denim shirt.

And then she saw him.

Standing at the heavy wooden entrance door to the castle. Silhouetted by the late-afternoon burnished gold sky.

Staring up at her.

She faltered mid-step, her heart dropping to

her steel-toecap boots and then catapulting back up into her chest.

Was it really him? After all these years?

Below her the idle chatter of the other staff died away.

Ten seconds later all hell broke loose.

'Your Grace! I had no idea… I understood from the estate office you were to remain at Bainsworth until the twenty-ninth, as is tradition.' Stephen, the head butler at Loughmore, was barely able to keep the panic from his voice.

Ciara just about managed to find the next step on the ladder before turning to face the scene unfolding below her.

All the crowd had shifted away from the tree to stand a respectful distance from him… Tom Benson… Eleventh Duke of Bainsworth. Under one arm he was carrying a scruffy-looking terrier, who was panting and wriggling in his eagerness to be let down.

The Duke had spent his childhood summers here in Loughmore, adored and indulged by all the staff. But he had not visited the castle for the past twelve years. The newer staff had never met him before, and even those who knew him seemed uncertain of how to greet him or even who they were dealing with.

For the briefest second he glanced up at her, those silver eyes giving nothing away. Ciara gripped the ladder rail even tighter, feeling completely off-balance. He still had the ability to make the world more vivid, more exhilarating, just by being in the same room.

He had changed. At eighteen he had been boyishly handsome, with brown hair deliberately too long and a restless energy that had never seen him stand still. Now his short hair only hinted at previous curls, and all that restless energy seemed to have been turned inwards, transforming him into a silent observer.

The intelligence in his eyes was sharper, his tall and lean athletic build more defined. The smoothness of his eighteen-year-old skin was gone, replaced by the hint of a five o'clock shadow and faint lines at the corners of his eyes.

His grey wool overcoat, gleaming black brogues and the dark suit underneath were in keeping not only with his title but also with his position as the owner of a chain of globally renowned restaurants that bore his name—Tom's.

The last time she had seen him he had been

wearing faded jeans and a crumpled polo shirt. He had caught the last flight from London to Dublin one late September night. Ciara flinched at the memory of that night and how they had argued. Across the hall she saw his shoulders stiffen even more, as though he was remembering that night too.

He flicked his gaze away from her and lowered his dog to the ground. It ambled away to sniff at a nearby pot plant. Then the Duke walked towards Stephen.

Both men shook hands before Tom…no, the Duke, as she needed to remember to call him now, said, 'My schedule changed and allowed me the opportunity to travel early. My mother, the Duchess, and my sisters want to spend Christmas here in Loughmore…' He paused before adding, 'Away from Bainsworth Hall.'

Uneasy silence descended as everyone reflected on the reason why that would be the case.

Then, clearing his throat, Stephen said, 'On behalf of myself and all the staff here at Loughmore, condolences on the death of your father.'

With a stiff nod of his head the Duke acknowledged Stephen's words. Then yet more awkward silence followed as everyone waited for the Duke to speak. To acknowledge their condolences or to explain why he was here earlier than expected. Perhaps even to explain why he hadn't visited Loughmore in years, or why it had taken him five months since his father's death to visit.

But instead he caught everyone unawares as he moved forward and began to introduce himself to the rest of the staff.

Libby was the first in line. She blushed and smiled and thrust a plate of gingerbread Santas in the Duke's direction. He declined her offer with a polite shake of his head.

Maggie, the head of Housekeeping, was next in line. Maggie had used to fondly scold the Duke as a teenager, for the endless mess he'd created around the castle—especially when he had friends to stay. Now she looked as though she wanted to hug him, as she had each summer when he'd arrived back from Eton. But the Duke held his hand out to her and formally they shook hands.

Forgotten by all and sundry—Sean and Libby having long neglected their promise to hold the ladder steady—Ciara had no option but to climb down on her own. Her already wobbly legs now felt truly un-coordinated. Her heart was unhelpfully lurching about her chest and the single loop-ing question in her brain was slowly driving her to distraction—what on earth was she going to say to him when they came face to face?

When she was nervous her default setting was to joke and make light of the situation. Some-times it worked, and defused the tension, but at other times it fell flat and she ended up looking like a complete fool. It was something she was trying to control, but it was hard to change a habit of a lifetime.

But maybe she was overthinking this. In all likelihood she was just a forgotten memory from his teenage years.

Long-buried memories accompanied each of her steps downward. Watching him cook in her gran's tiny cottage kitchen, where his inventive-ness as a chef had turned from a hobby into an all-consuming passion. Kissing him under the bridge at the far end of the lake, with the con-fined space, dim light and the trickle of water amplifying their laughter and chatter.

She remembered how Tom would climb to the top of the Japanese cedar in the Arboretum and dare her to join him... But even watching him forty feet off the ground had left her feeling giddy, and she would barely climb ten feet before giving up. And the way he would block out the sun when he leant over her as they'd lain in a mossy hollow they had found at the centre of Loughmore Wood, the affection shining from his eyes confounding her.

He had convinced her that the hollow had been created by a meteor. And it was there that her passion for native Irish plant species had begun. Later she would train to be a horticulturist, driven by the desire to preserve those plants and to conserve the historical importance of gardens such as Loughmore for future generations. Lying on that soft green blanket of moss, her hand in his, she had seen up close for the first time the intricate and delicate beauty of those often rare plants. Her gaze would shift from him to the breathtaking wonder of willowherb and Black Medick, and the world had been full of wonder and possibility and maybes.

But then reality would dawn and she would have to return to work. Dressed in her cleaning uniform, she would nod politely in his direction whenever they passed in the corridors of the castle, and he would do likewise in return. She'd tried to pretend to herself that she didn't care, but deep down the easy distance he was always so capable of had made her wonder at the truth of their relationship.

Lost in thought, she clambered down the ladder—but her lack of concentration caught up with her when she was less than six feet from the bottom. Her foot moved to connect with the next step down, but she must have overreached because suddenly she was feeling nothing but open air. With a yelp, she clung desperately to the ladder. But in slow motion she felt her whole body fall backwards, and then she was flying through the air.

Her only thoughts were of the hard marble floor about to greet her and the ignominy of her situation.

*Talk about making a holy show of yourself.*

But instead of feeling her bones crunching against a hard surface she fell into a solid grip.

Winded, she threw her head back in confusion to come really close to those silver eyes.

'You're still a terrible climber, I see.' His voice was a low rumble.

She tried to leap out of his arms, but they tightened around her. And she had to bite back the crazy temptation to say, *Welcome home, Tom, you've been missed.*

Cursing under his breath, Tom pulled the wriggling Ciara closer, trying to ignore the energy surge flooding his body at having her hip pressed against his stomach, her tumble of auburn hair softly tickling his wrist.

Other staff were starting to crowd around them, fussing over Ciara. He needed to make sure she was okay. He needed some space to think.

He shifted around and caught a horrified-looking Stephen's eye. 'Please bring tea to the morning room.'

He moved quickly away, Ciara still in his arms. Past the tapestries and family portraits lining the wide corridor. Not looking down. Trying to remember that he had come to Loughmore with one single purpose.

Boarding his private plane earlier that day, at the City of London airport, he had been determined to approach the next week logically. Even though he had done a double-take when he had seen Ciara's name as he'd glanced through the names of personnel employed at Loughmore that the estate office at Bainsworth Hall had sent through, he had remained determined that he was taking the right decision in returning to Loughmore and making the announcement that had to be made.

But as he had wound his way from the outskirts of Dublin city and into County Wicklow, the Garden of Ireland, past familiar landmarks— the rolling Wicklow mountains, the hidden lakes, the silent narrow roads with towering trees and road signs for ancient monuments, the Christmas lights threaded across the narrow main street of Avoca Village, the doors of the brightly painted terraced cottages wearing Christmas wreaths— something had shifted in him.

And when he had come to the brow of Broom Hill and Loughmore Castle had appeared below him in the valley he had pulled his rental car to the side of the road and climbed out. Standing on the edge of a ditch, in the fading light of a winter afternoon, he had buttoned his coat against the sharp breeze carried all the way in from the distant Irish Sea with bittersweet memories confounding him.

Loughmore Castle hadn't changed. It still sat proudly in the valley, its medieval tower standing pencil-sharp against the blue winter sky, the Victorian addition flanking it to the west, the Georgian courtyard to the rear. To the front of the castle sat Loughmore Lake, where Tom had learnt to sail and had had his first experimental kiss in the shadows of the boat house, with Hatta Coleridge-Hall.

To this day, his mother still dropped not so subtle hints that Hatta would make a good duchess.

It hadn't been until Ciara, though, that he had understood what a kiss should *really* be.

To the rear of the castle, beyond the walled garden and orchards, lay Loughmore Wood. The place where he and Ciara used to escape to, to talk and poke fun at each other at first and then, over the long weeks of that final summer together, to make love.

Standing there on the edge of that ditch, with the icy breeze whistling around him, he had winced at all those wonderful and sad and painful memories and he had known more than ever that he had come to the right decision on the future of Loughmore. It was time he put the ghosts of his past in Loughmore behind him for once and for all.

And as he had driven through the imposing

limestone arched entrance to the estate, and along the three-quarter-mile entrance avenue past the wide open fields, where deer were sheltering under oak and chestnut trees, he had been pulled back to his excitement as a child, when he had travelled to Loughmore each summer, relishing the freedom he'd got there, away from the ever-present sense of failure that had marked his schooldays.

His younger sisters, Kitty and Fran, had brought friends for company, and on occasions, to satisfy his parents' insistence that he 'socialise and network', Tom had too, but in truth he had wanted nothing more but to immerse himself in castle life. He had driven tractors, helped bring in the hay and milked the cows. He had spent hours with Jack Casey, the Yard Manager at Loughmore's stables, learning about horses, and even more hours in the kitchen with Jack's wife Mary, at first devouring her home baking and then, to his own surprise, cooking and baking himself under her guidance.

She had grown nervous about his visits, politely asking what his father would say, but he had charmed his way around her resistance. In time he had learned of his father's attitude to his passion for cooking but back then it had been his secret.

And then, one summer, Jack and Mary's granddaughter Ciara Harris had blown into the estate—like a turbo-charged breath of fresh air. Funny, outspoken, often unknowingly irreverent, she had questioned everything. And for the first time he had seen that his life could be different...

A fire was lit in the morning room, where table lamps cast faint shadows over the pale pink embossed wallpaper. Before the fire on a Persian rug was a footstool, still bearing the business and scientific journals and periodicals his father had insisted were to be ordered for all three of the estate's main properties—Bainsworth Hall, the two-thousand-acre main seat of the family in Sussex, Loughmore Castle, and Glencorr, the family hunting lodge in Scotland.

He lowered Ciara on to the sofa in front of the fire and stood back. Too late he remembered the time he had found her in here cleaning, and had dragged her giggling in protest to the sofa and kissed her until they were both breathless, hot with the intoxicating frustration of unfulfilled desire.

He shook away the memory and tried to focus

on the woman before him—not the girl he had once known 'Are you injured in any way?'

Immediately she stood and moved away from him, stepping behind the arm of the sofa as though that would shield her from him. She folded her arms and gave a wry shrug. 'Just my pride.'

For long moments they regarded each other, the crack and hiss of burning wood the only sound in the room.

Ciara tucked a lock of her long red hair behind her ear and rubbed her cheek. She rolled back on one heel. as though fighting the urge to move even further away. She regarded him warily and then, in a low voice, asked, 'How have you been?'

She'd always used to do this to him. Disarm him with the simplest of questions that left him floundering for an answer. How did you sum up twelve years?

'Good. And you?'

She tilted her head, the deep auburn tones of her hair shining in the light of a nearby Tiffany lamp and answered, 'Yeah, good too.'

A discreet knock sounded on the door to the room. Stephen entered, carrying a tray bearing a silver tea service and china cups. Storm bounded into the room behind him and jumped up on Ciara, his paws clawing at the denim of her black jeans.

He called to Storm, but the terrier ignored him as Ciara bent over and patted him, murmuring, 'Hello, cutie.'

Stephen placed the tea service on a side table, along with some delicate triangular sandwiches and some mince pies, before awkwardly considering Ciara. Then, clearing his throat to gain her attention, because she was still chatting with Storm, he said, 'If you are feeling better, Ciara, there is tea ready in the staff kitchen.'

Ciara straightened. Glanced in Tom's direction and then went to leave with Stephen.

Tom gritted his teeth. 'Stay and have tea here.'

Stephen did a poor job at hiding his surprise at Tom's words but, gathering up Tom's overcoat, simply asked, 'Would you like me to take your dog away, sir?'

'He's called Storm—and, no, he can stay here with me.'

After Stephen had left, Ciara motioned towards the door. 'I should go.'

'Why?'

'Staff don't have tea with the Duke.'

'I'm not my parents. I don't give a fig about what's the *done thing* or protocol. Now, have some tea and stop arguing with me.'

She looked as though she *was* going to argue with him, but then with a resigned shrug she went to the side table and poured tea into two cups, adding milk to one. Turning, she brought one of the jade-rimmed cups, with the family crest printed inside, to him.

Black tea—just as he had always drunk it. Was she even conscious that she'd remembered?

He gestured for her to take a seat on the sofa facing the fire, and took a seat himself on an occasional chair facing the bay window overlooking the lake.

Ciara watched as Storm settled on his feet, his belly lying as usual on Tom's shoes.

'Why did you call him Storm?'

'I didn't. He belonged to my ex-girlfriend. When she decided to return home to Japan I adopted him.'

Ciara said nothing in response. Instead she sipped her tea quickly.

Tom watched her, still thrown by seeing her after so many years.

They had once been so close. Ciara had been

the first person ever to ask what his dreams were, who had seen beyond his title and the expected path that had been mapped out for him from the moment he was born. It was Ciara who had encouraged him to follow his passion for cooking—who had challenged him to write to some of London's top restaurants seeking an apprenticeship. She had been the first person to believe in him. The first person who had helped him see who he *was* rather than who he was supposed to be.

But she was also the first person to have broken his heart; in truth the only ever person to do so. After Ciara he had been more circumspect in his relationships.

He could not go on reliving the painful memories of that time. It was time for closure.

Placing his teacup on a small walnut console table, he said, 'I understand your grandparents have retired?'

His question elicited a smile from her. 'Yes, they've moved back to County Galway. They bought a house in Renvyle—close to the beach. They love it there, but they miss Loughmore. Grandad especially misses the horses, and both miss the other staff. After working here for over fifty years leaving wasn't an easy decision for them.'

Years ago Tom would have understood why her grandparents missed Loughmore. He had once loved it more than any other place on this earth. But what had happened between him and Ciara had ruined his love affair with the castle. Now it represented guilt and shame and pain.

But did the fact that Ciara was working here mean that she had been able to bury the past? Was she unaffected by those memories?

'Is that why you're working here now—did you miss it?'

Ciara gave a non-committal shrug. 'I trained as a conservation and heritage horticulturist. Knowing how many rare Irish plant species there are at Loughmore, I applied for the gardening role that was advertised here during the spring of this year. You remember Sean? The head gardener?' When Tom nodded she continued. 'In the interview I told Sean about my interest in identifying and conserving the rare and threatened plants that are here. Thankfully he was interested in the project, and he also asked me to lead a programme to reintroduce heritage plants back onto the estate.'

'All those days in the woods…' Too late he re-alised his words.

Ciara flinched and looked into the fire, shifting her feet, clad in heavy boots, further beneath the sofa, as though she was trying to hide them.

In their last summer together, when they were both eighteen, their relationship had become much more than just friendship and flirting. It had started with a kiss in Loughmore Wood, as they had lain staring at the stars one July night. That summer had been wild and intoxicating. And special. They had made love several times. The first time for them both.

As the summer had drawn to an end, and he'd had to leave for his apprenticeship at one of London's Michelin-starred restaurants, Ciara for her horticultural course in Dublin, they had promised to stay in touch. See each other over term-breaks. It had been much too early to talk about a future together, but Tom had silently envisaged a time when they would be together for ever.

And then one day in late September, as he'd dashed from his apartment into the rain, late for work, he had crashed into Ciara as he'd rounded the corner of his street. Delighted, but thrown at seeing her standing on Kentish Town Road as the bus he needed to catch sailed by, he had simply stared at her when she'd told him she was pregnant.

He hadn't been able to take it in. He had muttered something about them working it out and that he had to get to work—that his head chef took pleasure in firing apprentices for being late. He'd given her the keys to his apartment. Promised to call her during his break.

Only hours later had he come to his senses. He had ignored the head chef's threats to fire him for leaving early and, despite the cost, had taken a taxi home. His father had refused to support him in his bid to become a chef, telling him it was 'beneath a Benson.' He had even threatened disinheritance. Tom hadn't known how he was going to support Ciara and a baby. But he'd known he would find a way.

His father's stance on Tom's career had summed up their relationship—he had never trusted Tom to make his own decisions, and dug his heels in when Tom went against his wishes. He'd pushed him further and further away, his disappointment and anger at Tom clear—so much so that since Tom had commenced his training they had rarely spoken to one another.

When he'd got to his apartment it had been empty. His frantic calls to Ciara had gone unanswered, so he had called a friend who'd got him to Heathrow within the hour. Just in time to catch the last flight to Dublin.

He'd gone to her mum's address. But the house had been empty. He'd waited on the doorstep and at one in the morning a taxi had pulled up. Ciara, pale and drawn, had emerged first, followed by her stony-faced mum. Ciara had refused to speak to him and both women had gone into the house, the front door slamming behind them.

An hour later the door had swung open again and her mother had whispered furiously, 'She'll talk to you for five minutes. No longer. This is to be the last time you ever see her. My daughter deserves someone better than *you*.'

He had tried to hold Ciara. To say he was sorry. But she had quietly told him she had miscarried and then asked him to leave.

When he had refused to go her expression had turned to one of contempt. And icily she had told him of her regret at sleeping with him. That she had made a stupid mistake she'd regret for ever.

He had returned to London, and despite the humiliation and guilt burning in his stomach at her rejection, at how he had failed her, he had called her several times a week for months. But she had never answered his calls.

Now, he looked up as Ciara stood, her fingertips working against a smear of dirt on her collar. 'I need to go and help with cleaning up after the tree installation.' She paused and bit her lip, and then, tilting her chin, asked, 'Can I meet with you tomorrow?'

'Why?'

'I'd like you to understand what we're trying to achieve with both the conservation and the heritage programmes I have introduced.' Her chin tilted back even further, and a hint of colour appeared in her cheeks. 'To continue with the programme next year we'll need a larger budget.'

He stood and walked towards the marble fireplace. The fire was burning out. He had planned on briefing the senior management at Loughmore first. But, given their history, and the way he had messed up everything all those years ago, the least Ciara deserved was his honesty.

Placing his hands behind his back, he squared his shoulders, turned back to her and said, 'I'm putting Loughmore up for sale.'

# CHAPTER TWO

FOR A BRIEF second Ciara hoped Tom was teasing her. Like he'd always used to do.

He had spent one whole summer trying to convince her that the entire dairy herd at Loughmore talked to him. Whenever they passed the grazing cows on their way to the woods he would stop and chat to them over the still-to-ripen blackcurrant laden hedges, relaying back to her what they were saying.

'Blue says it's going to rain later, but Nelly says Blue is talking rubbish. What's that, Nelly...? Ciara's looking beautiful today? Can't say I'd noticed it myself.'

At which point Ciara would give him a friendly thump on the arm and start pedalling her bike away, trying not to laugh, happiness bubbling in her chest at his words and at the way he would softly gaze at her when he said she looked beautiful.

But now there was no softness or laughter in his eyes.

She stepped towards him, murmurs of panic breaking through her disbelief. 'Sell Loughmore? Are you serious?'

He looked away from her and out towards the formal terraced gardens of Loughmore, rolling his neck from side to side. 'With my work commitments I rarely get the chance to come here. It doesn't make sense to hold on to the castle and estate.'

His voice was impassive, as though selling Loughmore was nothing other than yet another business deal to him.

Ciara moved away to the tea tray, staggered by just how devastated she felt by his casualness, by how little the castle meant to him. Her teacup rattled as she poured more tea. She could not let him see how upset she felt.

Loughmore was everything to her. Embraced not only by her grandparents, but also the rest of the staff, it had been a refuge from her lonely childhood in Dublin. It was where she had fallen in love for the first time...with the man so offhandedly telling her now he was selling it. The man she had lost her virginity to. The man who had created a baby with her, here on the grounds he was so indifferently about to sell.

Anger and deep upset fought for supremacy in her chest. She inhaled time and time again. Trying to calm down. Eventually she managed to say, 'Loughmore has been in your family for ever...you can't sell it.'

He glanced at her unhappily before walking towards the log basket at the side of the fireplace. 'There's no point in retaining a property that's never used.'

Seeing he was about to take some firewood and add it to the now-dying fire, she dashed forward and took hold of the log in his hand. 'I'll take care of the fire,' she said tersely.

She pulled at the log but he refused to let go. 'I'm perfectly capable of looking after it,' he said.

Ciara tried again to drag the log towards herself. 'It's not expected of you. I should have seen to it.'

With a heavy sigh Tom prised the log out of her grip, muttering, 'To hell with what's "expected".'

Bending, he lifted another log from the basket before walking back to the fire.

'I don't have the same old-fashioned expectations of my staff as my father did.' Throwing the logs onto the fire, sending a shower of sparks rising upward, he added, 'I thought you'd know that.'

Standing upright, he pulled off his suit jacket and threw it on the back of a nearby chair. His tie soon followed. Then he eyed her silently, his mouth set angrily, his shoulders squared, his hands propped on his hips.

They'd used to have stand-offs like this before. But back then Tom hadn't been quite so resolute. There was a harder edge to him now.

Ciara rolled back on her feet. She was unsure how to play this. He was the Duke now. She had to respect his position. But the anger and hurt inside her had her saying curtly, 'Those logs are smothering the fire—you need to set them at a more upright angle.'

Tom scowled at her. 'I didn't say I would do a good job of it, though, did I?'

And then for the briefest moment his mouth twitched.

Her heart took flight in her chest.

Oh, Lord, he was always irresistible when he smiled. His eyes would become magnetic in their silver sparkle and his wide-mouthed grin would swallow up everything that was wrong and horrible in the world.

But today the hint of that smile was nanosecond-brief before he turned back to the fire.

Ciara leant against the warm marble mantelpiece as he adjusted the logs with a fire iron. 'You're going to cause consternation amongst the staff if you change the way things are done around here.'

Hunkered down before the fire, he turned to her, those silver eyes holding hers. Softly he said, 'I'm selling Loughmore, Ciara.'

She winced at his words, but even more so at the heat that seeped through her body at the memory of how he'd used to whisper softly into her ear, telling her how much she meant to him. She'd used to laugh off what he said, calling him a chancer, terrified of believing him.

She moved away, taking care to skirt the antique Persian rug and cringing at her clumpy footsteps on the oak floorboards, thanks to her heavy work boots. She stood at the window on the opposite side of the room overlooking the walled garden. She had spent all summer working in there, reintroducing specimens that had been removed during an ill-judged replanting over forty years ago. What on earth would happen to the castle and its unique gardens and grounds if new owners took over?

Surely his mother and sisters weren't in agreement with him selling? They spent every summer and New Year here, and from what Ciara could tell they adored it. His mother was a remote and formal figure, who kept her interactions with staff to a minimum, but her affection and loyalty for Loughmore was clear in the way both she and the late Duke had carried out a thorough tour of every single part of the property each time they returned, making instructions on improvements and repairs to be made.

'What do your family think?'

'I haven't told them yet. I'll do so in the New Year.' He paused and frowned. Cleared his throat. 'A hotel consortium has signalled its interest in acquiring Loughmore.'

'Loughmore turned into a *hotel*! They'll change the castle beyond recognition. I've seen similar developments all over Ireland. They'll add on modern conference centres...build new homes and golf courses on the grounds. They'll wreck the place. Would you be happy to see Loughmore changed so utterly?'

'Things can't stay the same for ever—I'm sure whoever buys it will be sympathetic to its history.'

'I wouldn't be so certain. And have you thought about the staff? Loughmore and working for your family means *everything* to them.'

Tom gave an exasperated flick of his hand. 'That's why I'm here—I want to give them as much notice as I can. And I'll do my best to ensure they are all employed by the new owners'

'Working in Loughmore isn't just a job for the staff, though, it's a way of life. Many of them come from families that have worked on the estate for generations. They *love* Loughmore—they're immensely proud to work for your family.'

He considered her unhappily for long seconds and then gave a terse shake of his head. 'I'm holding a meeting with the senior staff tomorrow morning and I will brief all the other staff after that. The hotel group is keen for the sale to go ahead as soon as possible.'

'Can't it wait until after Christmas?'

'No. It's better the staff have as much notice as possible.' Moving towards the door he said, 'I have some work to do. I need to get my laptop from the car.'

'Stephen will have had it carried in already.' Pushing in front of him she added, 'Let me go and find out where he's put it—I suspect the library.'

She reached for the doorknob and pulled the door open an inch. But suddenly Tom was behind her, closing it with a push of his open palm.

For long seconds she stood with her back to him. He was wearing an aftershave she didn't recognise. But she did recognise the chain of reactions he caused whenever he came close—the thrill in her stomach, the inability to breathe, the heat that whipped through every cell in her body.

'Why are you acting like this?'

She jerked at his soft voice. Willed herself not to lean back into him.

Slowly she turned around. She breathed deeply against the impulse to reach out and run her thumb against his evening shadow...and then along the hard lines of his lips.

'Acting like what?'

His head tilted. 'As if you have to run after me...do every small task that I can do for myself.'

She hesitated, but then the question spilled out of her. 'Selling Loughmore...has it anything to do with what happened between us?'

He stepped back a bare inch, but it was enough to allow her to breathe.

His mouth tensed. 'Why would it?'

Twelve years ago, after the initial shock of discovering she was pregnant had worn off, she had naively hoped she and Tom would somehow cope. She had known it wouldn't be easy—they were both only eighteen, after all, with their own dreams and ambitions to follow. But her biggest mistake in her desperation to believe everything would be okay had been foolishly ignoring the fact that they were from different worlds, with families who didn't approve of what they believed was nothing more than a friendship.

*Know your place, Ciara. Don't be getting any notions.*

That had been her gran's constant refrain. It had used to drive her crazy—but no more so than the way she'd been treated by Tom's family, who didn't even seem to realise she existed as she went about her cleaning duties throughout the castle. She was a staff member, and she had been warned time and time again never to speak to a member of the family unless spoken to, and to leave a room if any of them entered.

When Tom had invited her to some social

events in the castle, his parents' disapproval had been obvious. As had his sisters' awkward embarrassment at having a member of staff in their midst. Their friendship had caused raised eyebrows not only in their families but also in the wider community.

One evening, at a recital that had been held in the castle, she had overheard two of the Duchess's friends talking.

"What does she think she's up to? Have you heard that accent of hers? As if a *Benson* would have anything to do with a working-class girl from Dublin."

No one but her mother had ever found out that they'd become more than friends. They had agreed to keep their relationship a secret. At first Ciara had been happy with that, but in their final weeks together, as they'd grown ever closer, the secrecy and lying had felt all wrong. It had felt as though she was living two separate lives—as though they were doing something shameful and what they had was nothing but a lie.

That day she had told him about the pregnancy she had flown home to Dublin early, unable to face any further humiliation. The sharp drawn-out pain in her stomach had started over the Irish Sea.

The moment she'd walked in the door of her mum's terraced house in Coolock her mum had instantly known something was wrong. She had taken her to the Rotunda Hospital, holding her hand for the entire taxi journey.

The fact that her mum had held her hand had freaked Ciara out—her mum wasn't given to demonstrative acts, and Ciara had known then that her baby was in serious trouble.

Later, after a young male doctor with sad eyes had gently told her she had miscarried, she had told her mum who the father was. Her mum had paled, called her a 'big eejit' and then turned away to stare out of the hospital window, before returning to her side and admitting her own relationship with Tom's father when she was Ciara's age.

Her mum had stumbled over her words, and the difficulty of confiding her secrets had been obvious in the anger in her eyes, the tension in her mouth. She'd only found out that Tom's father was marrying Lady Selena Phillips when it had been announced in the newspapers. She had called him at Bainsworth Hall. He'd eventually returned her call, incredulous that she hadn't realised they could never *possibly* have a future together, and telling her it was his duty to marry well.

Less than a year later Ciara's mum had married herself, after a rebound romance with a man who had subsequently walked out on them when Ciara was only a year old. Ciara's grandparents had disapproved of the marriage, and until she was a teenager there had been no contact between her mum and her grandparents.

Her childhood had been lonely. Her mum had worked long hours and Ciara had spent most evenings on her own. When her mum had come home, she'd always been too tired to talk, or to play with Ciara.

Her mum's confession that night in the hospital had been the first and only time her mum had opened up to her—allowed Ciara even a glimpse into her emotions. The default position in the Harris household was to be glib and pretend all was okay, to bury emotion beneath laughter and avoidance.

Now Ciara regarded Tom and wondered how he felt about everything that had happened all those years ago. A trace of humiliation still burnt brightly in her stomach, but mostly she just felt sad for the foolish and naive eighteen-year-olds they'd been then.

'You haven't been to Loughmore in twelve years.'

He blinked at her words. 'I've been busy.'

There was much she regretted about her relationship with Tom, but nothing more so than the way she had lashed out at him when he had come to her bedroom that night, pale and apologetic. It would be so easy not to talk about what had happened, but Ciara couldn't wish away just how close they once had been...those two naive eighteen-year-olds who had hurt one another so badly.

'That night in my mum's house... I was angry.'

A slash of red coloured his cheeks. 'You had a right to be.'

Ciara's heart squeezed tightly at the prideful tilt of Tom's head that did little to hide the emotion playing out in his eyes.

For the first time ever, when she and Tom had become lovers, she had let her guard down and ignored the Harris family motto of 'everything is fine'. She had told him her inner secrets, her loneliness and her guilt that her dad had left because of her, despite there being no evidence to back up that belief.

Tom had tried to persuade her to accept that she shouldn't feel responsible, but it still sat inside her—that feeling of being insignificant that came with having a father who had walked away from her for ever.

She had even embarrassingly admitted that she wanted to create a family of her own, with at least five children. Tom had teased her over that… but she had fallen even deeper in love with him when he'd said that she'd be the best mother ever. She had opened her heart to him. She had been stupid. Because doing so had only made his rejection—which she should have known was coming—a thousand times worse.

It was a mistake she'd never make again.

She looked at him now, sadness and regret bubbling in her throat. 'We should have just remained friends.'

His eyes held hers for what felt like for ever.

Eventually he nodded and said gently, 'Perhaps you're right.'

Overwhelmed by how emotional she felt, she stepped around him and collected his cup and saucer, placed them on the tea tray with her own, buying some thinking time in the process.

She liked her new life in Loughmore. Yes, she was occasionally caught unawares by a memory of Tom that rooted her to the spot. But she had long ago accepted that she needed to forge a life for herself. And through years of study and work in various conservation centres and heritage gardens, both in Ireland and Scotland, she had built a life she was proud of.

The conservation and heritage programmes she had started here in Loughmore needed to be continued. Loughmore itself needed to be saved from developers. And if that meant she needed to spend time with Tom, persuading him not to sell, then no matter how uncomfortable and awkward it would be she would do it—to save Loughmore.

She adjusted the tray in her hands and said, 'Don't tell the staff yet—let them enjoy Christmas.'

'I have to return to London on the first of January. I want to be here and available to talk through any concerns they may have.'

'Then plan on coming back in the New Year. You're only in London—it's not far to travel.'

He gave an unenthusiastic shrug and said, 'Perhaps.'

Her heart sank. He clearly wanted to spend as little time as possible in Loughmore. But, forcing herself to smile, she said, 'You never know—you might change your mind about selling over Christmas.'

His eyes narrowed. 'I have a buyer lined up. That's not going to happen.'

Ciara nodded. She needed to get Operation Save Loughmore underway immediately.

'The staff have organised a charity event in memory of your dad tomorrow night. Two hundred and fifty guests will be attending the turning on of the Christmas lights, with a choral concert and dancing later. I assume you'll attend?'

'I had forgotten it was taking place,' he answered, uninterested.

'But you'll come?'

'My father wasn't the easiest of men—it's a generous gesture by the staff.'

It was true. His father had terrified most of the staff in Loughmore. But at least he would never have dreamed of selling it.

Adjusting the tray in her hands, Ciara moved to

the door, which Tom opened to allow her to exit. Just as she was about to step out into the hallway she stopped and said, 'He was tough, but he commanded respect. He was loyal to Loughmore.'

Tom's mouth tightened. 'And I'm not?'

Ciara shrugged and said, 'I'm sure you have your reasons,' before walking away.

The following evening Tom half listened to the back-and-forth one-upmanship of the two opposing politicians who had collared him once the guests had moved from the tree-lighting ceremony and choral concert in the Great Hall into the ballroom for dancing. Several times he had tried to break away, but both men seemed determined to impress on him why he should consider becoming a supporter of their political party.

Not for the first time that night his gaze wandered once again over the invited guests in search of Ciara.

He took a slug of his Irish whiskey when he saw her still out on the dance floor with a guy he'd privately nicknamed Mr Brite, given his dazzling white smile. Wearing a knee-length red lace dress and towering heels, with her tumbling red locks worn loose and her sinful brown eyes full of laughter, she and Mr Brite twirled around the dancefloor.

Ciara looked like a fantasy Christmas present for every hot-blooded man. And she was a woman on a mission. It had taken him only a few hours today to cotton on to her plan.

After a lavish breakfast from Libby, Stephen had politely insisted he give Tom a tour of the castle, pointing out the renovations that had taken place in recent years and reminding him of the historical importance of the castle not only to County Wicklow but to the whole of Ireland.

Stephen had conveniently ended the tour in the courtyard, where Liam Geary, Loughmore's estate manager, had just happened to be standing by his estate vehicle chatting with Ciara. Before he'd known it Tom had been in the passenger seat, and Liam had taken him for a tour of the land, recounting his plans for extending the dairy herd and the possibility of introducing buffalo on to the estate.

On their way back to the castle they'd 'happened' to bump into Ciara again, this time chatting with her boss Sean at the start of the garden's Palm Walk.

'Wait until you see the orchard, sir,' Sean had

said with great excitement. 'We've expanded it greatly and we supply farmers' markets nation-wide. This year, thanks to Ciara's knowledge, we've planted new apple and plum saplings—they're old varieties that would have once grown here in Loughmore.'

Sean had then taken him on an extensive tour of the walled garden, the lakeside gardens and the orchards, breathlessly talking about his plans to extend the market garden.

His tour had ended at the glasshouses, where Ciara herself had taken him on a tour of the heritage plants she was cultivating.

He knew he had been cool with her throughout the tour—her jibe about his loyalty to Lough-more the previous evening had still been fresh in his mind. For a brief moment, when she'd said it, he'd wanted to tell her the truth. About how his father had left the estate in debt through poor financial investments. How selling Loughmore would significantly rebalance the books.

Tom had only learnt of the debts after his father's death. At first he had been angry—especially when he'd realised that his father had left it to *him* to inform his mother of the situation. Later he had felt nothing other than regret. A father and son should have had a better relationship. One with trust and mutual respect.

In the aftermath of his father's death Tom's resolve to value and cherish his own children, if he was ever to have them, had become all the more resolute.

Now, beside him, the politicians had moved on to a heated debate about land tax, and both became indignant when Tom interrupted to point out that their policies sounded remarkably similar and equally non-progressive.

Out on the dance floor Ciara turned to study him, before leaning towards Mr Brite and whispering something into his ear. Mr Brite turned and studied him too, before saying something to Ciara which, even in the low lights of the ballroom, Tom could see had made her blush.

Tom took another long slug of his whiskey, but the smooth tones of the ten-year-old blend were doing little to improve his mood.

With narrowed eyes he watched Ciara leave the dance floor and head in his direction. What was she up to now?

Beside him, the two politicians miraculously grew silent as Ciara approached them. Giving them her widest beam, she said, 'I'm sorry to break up your conversation, but the Duke promised me a dance earlier.'

Placing her hand on his elbow, she tugged him towards the dance floor. At first he resisted—but then he considered his options. The company of two self-important politicians or Ciara? She was the lesser of two evils. But only marginally.

He went with her, but at the edge of the dance floor he pulled her to a stop. 'Hold on—I believe we have a number of problems here.'

Ciara tilted her head and waited for him to explain.

'First off, I *didn't* promise you a dance.'

'You looked as though you needed rescuing.'

He'd give her that. 'Secondly, I don't think your previous dance partner will be too impressed with losing you.'

Ciara raised an eyebrow and pointed to the far end of the ballroom, where Mr Brite was surrounded by a group of women of varying ages, who were clapping along to his extravagant dance moves.

'Vince McNamara is the doctor in Loughmore now. His husband Danny is away skiing at the moment. He'll happily dance with anyone who admires his moves.'

'Which brings us to our third problem. You might not remember, but I can't dance.'

Amusement danced in her eyes. 'Oh, I remember, all right. But you need to get into the Christmas spirit.'

With that she dragged him out on to the dance floor. He shuffled along as she shimmied before him and the crowd around them bopped along to the band's rock 'n' roll rendition of another Christmas classic.

She gestured to him to take off his jacket, but he shook his head. Instead he leant towards her and said in a low voice, so only she could hear, 'I'm not going to change my mind about selling Loughmore.'

She shrugged and continued dancing, and then she leant towards him. 'So you said yesterday.'

She smelt of roses and vanilla. He tried to ignore the way her hips swayed along to the beat of the music. 'I'm on to you, you know.'

'What do you mean?'

'Libby's cooking, my tours of the castle and grounds today, then hot port and carols outside the front door at five. You're not going to change my mind.'

'They were all just coincidences.'

On the stage, the band segued into another song. This time it was much slower, and around them couples formed.

Ciara looked towards the stage with a frustrated frown and then gave him a bright smile, 'Well, I guess that's you off the hook.'

He should let her go. He knew he should. But all of a sudden he wanted to play her at her own game. As she moved to pass him he placed a hand on her waist and twisted her around, his other hand reaching for hers.

She tried to step away but he pulled her back.

She gave him a tight smile. 'I'm not sure this is appropriate. Us dancing together will have raised some eyebrows—slow dancing will set the cat amongst the pigeons.'

'You started it. Now, tell me what you've said to the rest of the staff.'

Blinking rapidly, Ciara protested, 'I've said nothing.'

He shifted nearer, stared her in the eye. 'Ciara...'

The two glasses of champagne she had drunk earlier were to blame. Ten minutes ago asking Tom to dance had seemed like an inspired idea. She wanted him to *enjoy* his Christmas in Loughmore, and he sure hadn't looked happy having his ear chewed off by two local politicians. But now that they were slow dancing that 'inspired idea' was quickly morphing into the worst decision she had taken in a very long time.

His hand enclosing hers was too familiar, too heart-stoppingly reassuring…too strong a reminder of how he'd used to touch her. His arm on her waist—heavy, in charge—was sending jittery shudders down the length of her legs. Pretending to be relaxed, to be unaffected by him, was already tearing her apart.

But what choice did she have? She had to save Loughmore. As her mum had always said, she needed to stop overthinking and just get on with it—preferably with a cheery smile on her face.

She craned her neck and met his gaze for a brief second, before shifting her eyes to the safety of the fine navy wool of his suit jacket. 'Okay… I'll admit I've said we need to make a special effort to make you feel welcome and part of the castle.'

She felt his muscles tense beneath the palm resting on his shoulder. In a low voice, much too close to her ear, he said, 'My life is elsewhere.'

Despite the hollow sensation that cracked in her chest at his words, she forced herself to keep her voice casual when she said, 'I think you'll regret selling Loughmore… Don't you want to pass it on to your heirs?'

His eyes duelled with hers while his hand on her waist shifted slightly, so their hips were now only inches apart. 'Who said there will *be* any?'

She raised an eyebrow. 'I bet you're beating back wannabe duchesses with a stick.'

A grin hovered on his lips. 'There *are* a few.'

'Bet your mum has a shortlist.'

All titled, beautiful, and with the right social graces, Ciara would wager.

Tom shrugged in response.

They moved around the dance floor, Tom awkwardly leading the way. His inability to keep to the beat of the music was rather endearing.

'Are you in a relationship?'

She looked up in surprise at his question. 'Not at the moment.'

'But you have been?'

It felt wrong to be talking like this with him. 'Kind of.'

'Meaning?'

'I've moved around a lot with my work. It doesn't lend itself to serious relationships. How about you?'

'I've had a few…but they haven't worked out. Now I'm too busy juggling my restaurants and the estate to find the time to sleep, never mind date.'

Her heart banged hard and furiously at the thought of him being with someone else. Even worse, a part of her wanted to know about every single relationship he had had. Had they been serious? Why had they broken up?

She bit the inside of her lip, and mentally gave herself a ticking-off. Why on earth would she do that to herself? She had to focus on saving Loughmore. Forget about the past.

'Loughmore will be a great summer home when you do eventually marry and have children. Remember how much you loved coming here?'

He shook his head but a smile glittered in his eyes. 'You're as persistent as ever, aren't you?'

He said it with such fondness that for a moment she forgot he was her boss, a member of the British aristocracy, the man who had once broken her heart.

His arm shifted on her waist and something darker, earthier entered his eyes.

She knew she should break her gaze away, but she couldn't. His eyes were so hypnotic, full of

intelligence, integrity and pride, but also a be-
guiling undercurrent of sensual suggestion.

A charge of dark, dangerous desire rippled in
the air between them.

He pulled her closer. She didn't resist.

'Tom—why didn't you *tell* us you were coming to Loughmore?'

Ciara jumped at the excited squeal behind her,
and Tom's arms floated away from her.

Turning, she had to step out of the way as a
blonde-haired woman dressed in black trousers
and a silver blouse, with a long grey cashmere
coat draped over her shoulders, moved in to hug
and air-kiss Tom.

Then, waving in the direction of the outside
terrace, beyond the row of French windows that
formed one wall of the ballroom, the woman
added, 'Tania and Jacob are outside, catching
up with Becky Johnson. They'll be back in a sec.
It's freezing out there, but they're huddled under
an outdoor heater, eating the toasted marshmal-
lows on offer from the outside caterers. What
fun! How fab to see you! We dined at Tom's in
Barcelona last month—the food was to *die* for.
Clever you!'

Ciara went to leave, but Tom called to her.

'Ciara! Let me introduce you to Amber Chamberlain.'

Amber turned and smiled at Ciara. 'Are you down from Dublin for the night too? Wasn't the traffic *horrendous*? That's why we're late. And they're predicting snow soon. It will be bedlam then.'

'No. I work here in the castle.'

'Oh.' For a moment Amber looked thrown, but she recovered well. 'Lucky you—working in such a lovely place.' Then she paused in thought. 'Wait a sec… I think I remember you.'

And then it dawned on Ciara. Tom had celebrated his eighteenth birthday here at Loughmore. He had invited her but the night had been a disaster, because she had known very few of the other guests and his parents had watched her unhappily all night. The following morning when she had come to work the party had still been going strong.

'The morning after Tom's eighteenth…' With a laugh, Amber held her hands to her cheeks. 'Do you remember, Ciara? You were cleaning in the games room and found me fast asleep on the billiard table. You helped me to my room.'

Ciara nodded, refusing to glance in Tom's direction. 'I remember now. Can I take your coat?'

'Please—and I would *love* a glass of champagne.' Turning to Tom, Amber linked her arm in his. 'Come on, let's go and find Jacob and Tania. They'll be dying to chat with you. They're off to St Moritz tomorrow. Will you be there as usual this New Year?'

Tom did not move, despite Amber's best efforts to lead him towards the terrace. 'Ciara, why don't you join us?'

Ciara saw the flicker of confusion on Amber's face. No doubt she was wondering why Tom was asking one of the staff to socialise with them.

All those years ago as a teenager she had been pretty much blind to the social wall that existed between herself and Tom. Youthful enthusiasm, idealism, naivety... Call it what you will, it had had her believing their different backgrounds didn't matter.

All that innocence had ended on the day she had travelled to London.

She gestured towards the dance floor. 'I need to get back to Vince... I promised him we'd have another dance together.'

Moving through the crowd, she took Amber's

coat to the temporary cloakroom that had been set up in the library. The two teenage girls from the village who had been employed for the evening to man the cloakroom jumped up when she entered, frantically trying to hide their phones.

She hid her amusement and said, 'Kelly, come with me to the kitchen, I need to organise drinks for some guests, and you two look as though you could do with some of Libby's baking to get you through the next few hours.'

In the kitchen, as Kelly filled a plate with Libby's delicate savoury pastries and mini-Christmas puddings, Ciara directed one of the waiters to take a bottle of champagne and glasses out to the terrace. Then, seeing how exhausted Libby was, she forced Libby to sit down while she made her a pot of tea.

*Know your place.*

There was actually wisdom in that saying. When her gran had used to say it to her she'd seen it as a putdown. But in fact her gran had only being trying to protect her. She had seen what unrealistic dreams had done to her mother— bringing a pain and humiliation that were hidden behind a wall of defiance and avoidance and a family rift that had gone on too long. Now she understood how worried they must have been when they'd seen history about to repeat itself.

They had only been trying to protect her from her own foolishness and naivety.

This time around she knew her place.

# CHAPTER THREE

THE FOUR-BY-FOUR SLEWED towards the hedge on the narrow road. Tom steered into the skid, feeling the car scraping against brambles and seeing a shower of snow thumping against the side windows before he finally managed to bring the vehicle to a stop.

He switched off the engine. The fresh snow on the side of the vehicle slid to the road with a thud and then there was nothing but absolute silence. Nothing stirred. Not a single bird was to be seen in the early-morning milky blue sky. Not a cry nor a bleat from an animal. It was as if the earth was having a sleep-in, having exhausted itself in the intensity of the snowstorm that had hit the east coast of Ireland the previous night.

Below him in the valley the vibrant emerald fields of Loughmore had disappeared under a blanket of sparkling white snow. Switching the engine back on, he crunched his way through the snow-covered perimeter road of the estate, where the high limestone wall to his right marked the boundaries with the neighbouring farms. After a few minutes he finally caught a glance of his last destination for the morning: Butterfly Cottage.

It was nestled in a copse, and he could just about make out its thatched roof beneath the snow.

He drove down the long incline into the heart of the valley, the four-by-four skidding on the more sheltered parts of the road. Last night, the initial flourish of snow had frozen hard, to be followed later by a heavier and more prolonged snowfall.

At the cottage, the garden gate refused to budge, so he had no option but to leap over the low wall that surrounded the property, built to stop the estate's cows and sheep from wandering into the garden.

On the other side of the wall he muttered to himself as he landed into a particularly deep snow drift and snow flooded the inside of his wellington boots.

His knock on the rose-pink-painted cottage door echoed into the valley. He had to knock a second and then a third time before the door swung open.

Dressed in a fluffy yellow dressing gown, her

hair mussed up and her cheeks pink, Ciara stared at him through sleepy eyes. 'Tom… I mean, Your Grace, what are you doing here?' Then, pausing, she peered over his shoulder. 'Oh, my God! I can't believe how much snow there is.'

Her eyes grew wide and her gaze shot back to his.

'My alarm didn't go off! I slept in! I'll be up at the gardens as soon as I can. I know snow was forecast, but I hadn't realised so much would fall. I don't usually work on a Sunday, but I would have been up inspecting the gardens earlier if I had known.'

'I'm not here because I expect you to be at work.'

'Why are you here, then?'

'The electricity in the castle went out overnight. The emergency generator took over—'

Ciara interrupted him, her expression alarmed, 'Were the outside buildings affected? The greenhouses?'

'No, they're all okay.'

She gave a grateful exhalation and then with a deep shiver added, 'It's Baltic out here—come inside before we both perish.'

The living room of the cottage was directly inside the front door. A Christmas tree, laden down with decorations, sat in one corner. Christmas cards were strung over the mantelpiece, and an array of angels and Santa Clauses and reindeers were spread on every other available surface.

Moving over to the small cottage window overlooking the front garden, Ciara leant down and propped her elbows on the deep windowsill. She shook her head as she stared at the wintry scene outside. 'I have never seen so much snow. Thank God we covered some of the more vulnerable plants with fleeces.'

There was a light switch to one side of the front door. Tom switched it to on. The brass light at the centre of the room remained unlit.

Ciara gave a groan. 'Oh, seriously… No wonder my radio alarm didn't go off.'

'You're not the only one. I've called in to all the other estate cottages this morning to make sure everyone is okay—several others are without electricity too. You're the last on my list, being the furthest out. I'd hoped you wouldn't be affected too.'

Ciara looked at him in surprise. 'You've called in to every cottage? How did everyone react?'

Now that he thought about it, his arrival *had*

caused a certain level of consternation in each of the cottages. 'They were a little thrown, I suppose. What's the problem with me calling?'

Beneath her yellow dressing gown she was wearing old-fashioned white cotton pyjamas, with a lace detail running down the front of the top, the bottoms ending at mid-calf, with yet more lace detailing. The cute pyjamas and fluffy dressing gown, her mussed up hair and rosy skin, along with the remaining heat in the room from last night's fire, all combined to give him the strangest urge to take her in his arms and hold her. Inhale her sleepy scent.

He glanced away from her.

'Calling in to the cottages…it's not something your dad would have done,' Ciara said gently.

'No, I don't suppose it is.'

She regarded him as though she were trying to understand him, and then a soft smile broke on her lips. 'It's a thoughtful thing to do, though.'

Warmth seeped through him at her smile. An alarming tightness gripped his heart.

He tried to refocus. 'What will you do? Is there someone you can stay with until the electricity is restored?'

'It's okay—I'm leaving later today anyway, to

spend Christmas with my mum. After I've helped out at the kiddies' party at the castle. Hopefully the electricity will be restored before I get back.'

'The road out of Loughmore is impassable.'

Her mouth dropped open. 'Oh, for crying out loud!'

'Liam Geary rang the council. They won't be able to clear the road before Christmas Day.'

'So we can't get out?'

'Nor people in to Loughmore. The weather has hit the south of England too. My mother and sisters are having to postpone their journey until after Christmas.'

Ciara leant against the windowsill, her eyes wide. 'That's terrible.'

'My mother accepts it's outside her control... and I think it might actually help her to stay at Bainsworth. It may be painful, as it's the first Christmas without my father, but at least there she has happy memories of past Christmases. And I'm sure they'll make it in time for the New Year Eve's ball. What will you do now that you can't get to Dublin?'

Ciara shrugged. 'I'm not sure... I'll chat with Libby. She's working on Christmas Day. I might go and spend it with her at the castle.'

'I've told Libby and the other staff who were scheduled to work over Christmas to take the time off. They're staying to run the children's party later today but then taking Christmas Eve through to Boxing Day off.'

'But that means you'll be in the castle completely on your own for three whole days.'

'I was hardly going to get them all to come in to look after *one* person. I'm sure they would all much prefer to be at home with their families.'

'But what will you *do*?'

Tom could not but help laugh at the horror in Ciara's eyes. 'Work. Cook dinner for myself. Up until this year I've spent a decade looking after myself—apart from a cleaner who comes in a few days a week. I can perfectly manage without staff.'

'But that's no way to spend Christmas Day. Christmas should be about having fun and sharing it with others. Creating memories.'

He wasn't going to admit it to Ciara, but part of him was glad it had snowed. At previous Christmases he had felt duty-bound to spend it with his family. Invariably he'd leave early, feeling claustrophobic because of his father's unending silent scrutiny and his mother's recounting the tale of yet another classmate of his who had married recently. His sisters were no better, in their mission to set him up on blind dates with friends and acquaintances of theirs.

Tom had never told any of them, because he knew they would only make his life hell, but he had no interest in dating *or* relationships. His last relationship had been over two years ago, with Maki—Storm's first owner. As with every other previous relationship of his, it had ended in rows, with Maki accusing him of being too remote, too closed.

What was it she'd said? 'I've never known you, Tom. I've never understood what's in your heart.'

Cancelling Christmas at the castle was also a relief to him because he'd much prefer not to have the guilt of having the staff he was soon going to have to tell that their jobs might be redundant waiting on him on Christmas Day.

'My work means that I rarely get time to myself. I'm looking forward to having some downtime and space to think. But what about you? Have you someone to stay with?'

She gave him a hopeful look. 'Maybe the electricity won't be off for long—the suppliers won't want people spending Christmas without it.'

'Liam called the supplier. Until the road into Loughmore is clear they won't be able to repair any of the lines.'

Ciara's expression fell.

Drained after a night of virtually no sleep, he went to sit on the armrest of the yellow-and-white-striped sofa that sat in front of the fireplace. He had barely placed his hand on the armrest when he snatched it away again, jumping at the angry hiss that emanated from a dark corner.

'What was *that*?'

Clearly amused, Ciara moved in front of the sofa. Popping her hands on her hips, she stared down into the corner. 'You *must* behave, Boru.' Looking back at him, she said, 'Sorry about that. Boru is especially cranky with any man who calls.'

Tom dared to peer over the armrest. A jet-black cat with bright green eyes stared back at him and hissed again, before slowly uncurling and leaping from the sofa. He slunk by Ciara's legs and climbed the stairs of the cottage with an indignant toss of his head.

Shaking her head, Ciara stared after the retreating cat. 'God, he's the most contrary cat ever—he never does anything I ask of him.' Turning in the direction of the kitchen, to the rear of the living room, she glanced at the multi-coloured cuckoo clock sitting over the sink. 'I'd better get a move on. Sean and the rest of the gardening crew are on annual leave. I'm the only one still on the estate.'

'Back to my question—where are you going to stay until the electricity is restored?'

She grimaced. 'I don't know. Libby is allergic to cats, and all the other staff who live on the estate have families of their own. I don't want to intrude on their Christmases.'

'How about your friend Vince?'

'God, no—his Tiger tried to take a lump out of Boru the last time they met.'

'Tiger?'

'Vince's Jack Russell.' She shrugged 'I have plenty of firewood, and as the go-to or birthday present for any woman over twenty-five seems to be a smelly candle, I have enough of them to last me a lifetime. I'll be fine here.'

'But you can't stay here without electricity.'

She raised an eyebrow. 'Humankind survived without electricity for millennia. I'm sure I'll cope.'

He stared at her, the inevitable offer on the tip

of his tongue. But he was loath to say it. Spending Christmas alone with Ciara was the last thing he wanted to do. There were too many memories, too much attraction, too much unfinished business still between them that he didn't want to rake up.

But he couldn't leave her here on her own—not when he had a whole castle to himself. He inhaled a long, deep breath. 'Come and stay in the castle.'

Ciara's mouth dropped open. She eventually managed to say, 'No… Thank you, but I don't… I can't…'

He pulled off his coat, rested it on the back of the sofa. 'Your car won't make it through the snow. I'll wait while you change and pack.'

Her eyes narrowed and she folded her arms defiantly. 'I *love* Christmas—I'll want to do all the traditional things…opening presents, the full works at dinner, playing games after. Are you prepared to take part in all of that?'

'I hadn't planned—'

She interrupted him. 'I'll stay here, in that case.'

He gave her a stern look, in no mood to debate this. 'Look, it makes sense—I have acres of space in the castle, and at least there you'll be closer to the gardens in order to take care of them.'

She considered that for a moment. 'That's true.' She paused, as something seemed to dawn upon her. 'And as you've told the rest of the staff not to work I can look after *you*.'

'I don't need looking after.'

She just shrugged, clearly not accepting that he did not require any help in the castle over the next few days.

Tense already, from the testing driving conditions earlier and now from this stand-off with Ciara, he stretched his arms over his head to ease the tension in his shoulders.

Ciara ran her gaze over his body, her eyes growing wider and wider as they travelled down his chest, pausing at his abs then skimming over his hips. Heat blasted in her cheeks.

'I...' She paused, backed away towards the stairs, 'I need to get changed.'

'We're not finished with our conversation.'

To that she just shrugged again, before turning and darting up the stairs.

He closed his eyes. Sucked in some air.

There was still a spark between them. A dangerous spark. Which meant that inviting her to the castle was risky. But he couldn't leave her all alone. He owed it to her.

It was up to him to control what was happening between them...not to do anything that they would later regret.

She had been right when she'd said they should have just stayed friends. In loving Ciara he had opened himself up to another person for the first time in his life. It had been both intoxicating and terrifying.

Through gentle teasing she had drawn him out. For years he had disappointed his parents, felt the heavy weight of their disapproval and frustration at his end-of-term reports and frequent school meetings to discuss his lack of academic progress. He knew he wasn't the son they had hoped for—an all-rounder academic and sportsperson in the mould of his father.

Ciara had been the first person who'd accepted him for what he was. But he had failed her. When she had rightly cut him out of her life he'd thought *his* life would be empty and grey for ever. It had taken him years to put the pieces of his shattered heart back together again. He could never relive that pain. Even being near her now was bringing back unwelcome memories and thoughts of what might have been.

In an alcove beneath the stairs sat an old writing desk, its central green leather writing surface faded with time. On the dark wood surrounding the leather there were at least a dozen framed photos of Ciara. He picked one up, and then another.

Some were of Ciara standing with people who looked like colleagues in various garden settings. In all of them she was at the centre of the group, her arms linked tightly around the waists of those standing beside her. She looked buoyant and proud in them all. Others were holiday photos—Ciara sitting in the sun with friends, with elaborate cocktails, and a winter snap of a boat ride in Amsterdam. Another showed her wading out of an azure sea, wearing a black bikini, one hand on her forehead pushing away her wet hair.

He breathed in deeply and turned away from the image of her in the bikini.

He stared at the long row of Christmas cards over her mantelpiece. No doubt from friends and colleagues. She had led a full life since he had last seen her. He admired her for what she had achieved. Why, then, did it leave him feeling so unsettled?

He was standing at the kitchen sink, filling a glass of water when Ciara reappeared.

Wearing a silver turtleneck Christmas jumper adorned with glistening white stars, which skimmed the waistband of her tight-fitting black jeans, she looked cute and as sexy as hell.

Her gaze fell to the half-eaten cookie in his hands. He had found a tray of cookies lying on the kitchen counter and, not having eaten anything all morning, had been unable to resist taking one.

Ciara grimaced at the cookie and then darted to the fridge. 'I should have offered you something to eat before I got dressed. Would you like a sandwich? I can't offer you a hot drink...' she turned with a carton of apple juice '...but how about some juice?'

'Water is fine...and I couldn't fit in another bite after this cookie. It's rather filling.'

She gave him a disbelieving look before pouring some juice into a glass. He watched her sip it, trying to get a grip on the way her behaviour with him kept swinging from one extreme to another. Sometimes she was her old forthright self and then at other times she became almost deferential. Something was going on that he wasn't grasping.

Taking a sip of the ice-cold water, he said, 'I didn't see you again after our dance on Friday night. You didn't join Vince as you said you would.'

There was something about Tom's tone—an edge to it—that had Ciara pausing in placing the cap back on the juice carton. She glanced over at him, and then away. Did he *have* to stand there in her kitchen wearing such a tight-fitting tee shirt? She tried to shake off the image of the six-pack he had earlier exposed when he had stretched. His long sleeved grey tee shirt had parted from jeans that hung sexily low on his hips to reveal spectacular abs...

'I ended up helping Libby in the kitchen,' she said.

'Why? It's not your job.'

'She needed help. I didn't mind.'

'Why wouldn't you join myself and Amber?'

She knew by his tone that he wasn't going to let this drop. Twisting the cap good and tight on the carton, she put it back into the fridge. Closing the fridge door, she leant against it, suddenly feeling a little dizzy.

Should she just leave well alone? Leave the past where it belonged? But something deep inside her was telling her that Tom deserved to know. Especially as he was inviting her to stay in the castle for Christmas.

Ciara liked to think that she wasn't a coward, but the thought of being stuck out here all alone in the cottage in the pitch-darkness of a winter's night was pushing her towards accepting his invitation. That and the fact that staying with Tom over the Christmas made sense in terms of her campaign to save Loughmore. She could use the time they spent together to persuade him not to sell.

But first there were things he deserved to know.

She swallowed hard and asked, 'Your dad and you…? How were things between you in recent years?'

Tom's eyes narrowed and his mouth turned downwards. He gave a shrug that was nothing but casual. 'He had come to accept who I am.'

It didn't sound as though his father had lowered his unrealistic expectations. 'Was he proud of everything you've achieved with your restaurants?'

Tom rose an eyebrow. 'A double Olympian horseman with a first from Cambridge has very high standards.'

For a moment Ciara closed her eyes, and then in a rush she said, 'I think there's something you should know.'

He looked at her blankly.

'Your dad and my mum…' She paused and inhaled a steadying breath. 'Well, they…they had a relationship when they were teenagers. It ended when they were both twenty-one. They kept it secret…just like us. My mum only knew it was all over when she read about his engagement to your mum in the newspapers.'

Tom dropped his glass to the counter with a thud. '*Your* mum and *my* dad!'

Why did he sound so appalled? 'Don't you think she was good enough for him?'

Tom stepped away from the counter and threw his arms up, looking at her as though she had lost her mind. 'What are you *talking* about? When did I say that?'

Taking her by surprise, anger on behalf of her mum fizzed through Ciara. Fiercely she countered, 'My mum was heartbroken. She met my dad and married him soon after. And we both know how *that* ended—with him upping sticks when I was only a year old.'

Tom grimaced. Stepped back. Lowered his head from her gaze for a beat to study the quarry-tiled floor of her kitchen. Inhaling deeply, he looked back up at her, grim-faced. 'I'm sorry about what my father did to your mother.'

His apology sounded genuine...even heartfelt. It doused her anger, and in a low voice she said, 'I thought you should know... It explains so much. Especially why your dad was so opposed to us being friends.'

Tom's mouth tightened. '*And* why your grandfather in his very polite and roundabout way asked me to stay away from you.'

'Did he?'

Ciara could not keep the surprise from her voice. Her grandad was a reserved man, who kept himself to himself. Like her grandmother, he was a traditionalist and had always believed in respecting the family they served—which included never commenting on them or their behaviour. For him to have said anything to Tom must have meant that he had been extremely worried.

Ciara felt a pang of guilt for the anxiety she must have caused her grandparents. Only now, with hindsight, could she appreciate the dilemma they must have faced back then, with their desire to spend time with their only grandchild versus seeing her following a destructive path similar to her mother's.

'I respected your grandfather. I didn't like going against his wishes.'

Ciara's heart skipped a beat at the obvious toll it had taken on Tom to go against the wishes of her grandad—a man she knew he was fond of. 'Why didn't you tell me?'

'He asked me not to say anything to you. He said he knew I would do the right thing and not hurt you.'

At that Tom stopped and held her gaze. Silence settled around them. She bit her lip, trying to ignore the ache in her chest. She had moved on from all this years ago. Hadn't she?

She grabbed a tea towel and reached for the mixing bowl that was still lying on the draining board from when she had made the cookies last night. Tom had unfortunately decided to test them. She hoped for his sake he had a strong stomach.

Drying the bowl with quick wipes, she said, 'My grandparents tried to stop my mum from seeing your dad. They knew it could never last and how infatuated she was with him.'

Opening her baking cupboard, she placed the bowl on the base of her food mixer.

Then, catching his gaze, she said quietly, 'But you know…first love—it's dangerously powerful, unfortunately.'

She turned away from him, seeing his expression grow even tighter and picked up a tablespoon from the draining board.

'My mum hated the fact my grandparents had been right in their warnings and felt betrayed by their decision to remain employed here,' she added. 'But my grandparents felt huge loyalty towards your grandfather, who was then Duke, and it was also a time when there wasn't much employment in Ireland. In reality they didn't have much choice *but* to stay here. My mum was all against me staying with them every summer. And now I understand why. They were always warning me about getting too close to you. They must have been really worried about history repeating itself.'

Tom rinsed his glass, saying nothing.

Ciara tried not to glance at his easy movements,

the way his hard muscles flexed beneath his tee shirt.

He turned and held her gaze, those silver eyes shadowed. 'My family has a poor record in how we have treated yours.'

Ciara's heart fluttered at his softly spoken words. 'I'd like to think it's all in the past now. We've all made mistakes.'

'Come and stay at the castle.'

'Are you sure that's a good idea?'

'Considering you're going to be bringing that crazy cat with you, maybe not… But it's time my family started doing the right thing by yours—starting with me offering you a place to stay this Christmas.'

The gentleness, the honesty and integrity in Tom's voice, in his steady and proud gaze, had Ciara closing her eyes for a second. Opening them again, she said, 'I don't want there to be tension between us… If I stay in the castle can we just leave the past behind us and enjoy Christmas?'

Tom considered her words for a while, his jaw working. Then with a nod he said, 'When I leave in the New Year I'd like us to part as friends.'

Ciara tried not to blush at the implications of his words. 'Of course!'

She gave him a wobbly smile, trying to ignore the stupid hurt and disappointment inside her that that was all he would ever see her as. A friend. Nothing more.

Of course he was right.

She knew that.

It was just that her heart was having a hard time catching up with the logic of the situation, with the understanding that this was nothing more than two old friends spending Christmas together. But it was the best way to get through all of this.

'I'll go and pack.'

She was halfway up the stairs when he called out, 'I'm not sure Storm's going to be impressed with Boru, though.'

He had a point. But if she was going to spend the next few days trying to pretend that Tom Benson had no effect on her, whilst also trying to persuade him to keep Loughmore, Storm and Boru would have to do their bit and learn to get on.

'I'm sure they'll get on famously,' she said. And then she heard herself say with a laugh, 'Just like us.'

Tom raised his eyes heavenwards.

Ciara darted up the rest of the stairs, trying

to convince herself that staying in the castle all alone with Tom was not a big deal.

Unfortunately it didn't work.

# CHAPTER FOUR

ON A CALL to Oliver Browne, Tom's Edinburgh restaurant manager, Tom shook his head in exasperation as he heard about the flu that had wiped out half of Oliver's staff over the past few days.

Oliver had contained the crisis by recruiting temporary agency workers to replace his ill staff, but it was far from ideal. The success of Tom's Restaurants was not based only on their innovative menus, that used the best-quality regional produce, but also on the exceptional quality of service every customer who walked through the doors of Tom's received.

Tom had made it mandatory that all staff members had to attend a two-day in-house customer care course to ensure they all followed the service standards he expected.

Listening to Oliver's briefing on the fall-out of trying to run the restaurant without his usual staff at this peak time for the restaurant trade, Tom realised not for the first time that trying to run both the estate and his restaurant business in parallel was going to be a challenge—and yet another reason why selling Loughmore was the correct decision.

His phone tucked under his chin, he twisted around in his chair when he heard the library door open.

Three tiny heads peeked around the doorframe.

Spotting him at his desk, the little girls gave a high-pitched squeal and disappeared. Much giggling outside the door followed, and then the sound of a familiar voice.

He finished his call with Oliver just as Ciara entered the room, beckoning a reluctant trio in behind her.

He raised an eyebrow in Ciara's direction, his mouth twitching at the knee-length 'Mrs Claus' dress she was wearing, red velvet with white trim. Her hair was plaited to the side, and on her head she wore a matching red velvet white-trimmed hat.

Ciara threw him an unamused look. 'This was *not* my idea. Blame Libby—she's the main organiser of the kiddies' party this year and she insisted we all dress up.'

Shaking his head, he turned his attention to the

three little girls whom he guessed were roughly five years old and were now staring at him wide-eyed.

Dressed in identical long-sleeved black velvet dresses, with pink and white embroidered Celtic designs on the front panel and along the base of their short flared skirts, the girls wore tiny black soft-soled dance shoes on their feet, and their loose hair was held back by black velvet bands.

'These girls are here for the party, and as they dance with the local Irish Dancing school they're taking part in a dance display for us later. They were keen to meet you, so I said we'd drop in for a few minutes to say hi,' Ciara said, by way of explanation for their unplanned visit.

Preoccupied by his call with Oliver, and the workload he needed to get through this afternoon, Tom felt a flicker of irritation—but even he was unable to resist the shy but excited trio staring at him as though he was the eighth wonder of the world.

'Hi, girls.'

The three giggled once again.

Walking to his desk, Ciara gestured for the girls to follow her.

When they came to stand directly in front of

him he held his hand out to them. Reluctantly they shook it, giggling when he said to each one, 'Very nice to meet you, Miss Irish Dancer.'

'We're not called Miss Irish Dancer!' replied the raven-haired leader, who had been the first to enter the room and the first to dare to walk up to his desk at Ciara's beckoning.

'Really? So, what *are* your names?'

'I'm Grace,' said the raven-haired spokesperson.

'I'm Sophie,' said her little friend with long bright red hair and a heavy dusting of freckles.

'And...and I'm Grace too,' stammered the shyest of the three, her hands nervously twisting the heavy velvet fabric of her flared skirt.

'Hello, Grace Two.'

She shook her head, her blonde curls bobbing up and down. 'No, I'm just Grace.'

Tom leant back in his chair and slapped his forehead. 'Silly me. Hello, Just Grace.'

The three girls leant into one another, giggling even more at his foolishness.

Ciara considered the laughing trio fondly and then, meeting his eye, gave him a grateful smile. The girls' light and delicate laughter danced around the room and something unexpected shifted inside him at hearing their joy, seeing the amusement dancing in Ciara's eyes.

In that moment it hit him just how much he had missed the thrill of doing something to make her happy. How had he spent the past twelve years not realising that? Now, sitting in the library of Loughmore, seeing her brown eyes twinkle, and the way she placed a hand on her chest bone when something entertained her, the life he had led for those twelve years felt as though it belonged to another person.

He gritted his teeth, glad now that he had said he wanted them to part as friends earlier, in her cottage. Making that statement out loud to Ciara had been an insurance policy against him doing anything stupid around her.

Like kiss her.

Especially in light of how despicably his father had treated her mum.

Plopping her arms on his desk, Grace One studied him with a hint of wonder. 'Are you really a prince?'

'Not a prince. I'm a duke.'

'What's a duke?'

'Well… I suppose I'm like a cousin to a prince.'

Grace One shook her head and looked at him, unconvinced. 'You look like a prince to me.'

'Yes, you look like the Prince in my *Sleeping Beauty* book,' Sophie added in a determined tone.

'*And* you live in a castle,' Grace Two added, and then, shyly tugging once again on the fabric of her skirt, she added in a whisper, 'It's so beautiful…' She pronounced beautiful '*beaut-fil*', and his heart melted at the blush that formed on her cheeks when he smiled at her.

But her two friends continued to study him unhappily, as though convinced he was holding back on admitting that he really was a prince.

He looked helplessly in Ciara's direction. She bit her lip, clearly fighting to hold back laughter. He eyeballed her. It had been her idea to bring the girls to visit him—the least she could do was help him out.

Clearing her throat, Ciara bent down beside his desk and looked towards the three girls. 'A duke is just as special as a prince, girls. And *our* Duke is extra-special because he is also a very famous chef, who performs magic in the kitchen. People all over the world love his work. I think that's even cooler than being a prince, don't you?'

Thrown by the pride in Ciara's voice, Tom shuffled in his seat. He frequently received positive critical reviews of Tom's Restaurants, but to hear Ciara's words felt a thousand times more gratifying.

He cleared his throat, taken aback by the sudden lump that had formed in his throat. It had been Ciara who'd encouraged him to follow his dreams to be a chef. She had seen the buzz he got from creating new dishes, the pleasure he found in the delight he evoked in people when they tasted his food. She had understood his desire to create a name for himself, independent of his title—his need to prove to his father that he could be a success in his own right, that he wasn't going to be a failure all his life.

And for the past twelve years, no matter how much he tried to deny it to himself, every career step he had taken had also been about proving to *her* just what he was capable of. But even though her praise was pleasing, it was also disturbing... He shouldn't care so much of what she thought of him.

Pushing those thoughts away, he focused on the girls. Ciara's words seemed to have taken away some of their disappointment that he wasn't a prince as they were once again regarding him with renewed enthusiasm.

Grace One propped a hand under her chin and asked, 'Have you met the Queen?'

'Yes, many times.'

In unison, all three whispered, 'Wow...'

'How about Cinderella?' Sophie asked, with hope gleaming in her eyes.

'No, not yet. But maybe some day I will.'

'Will you marry her?'

This was worse than an interrogation from any journalist. He looked in Ciara's direction. A flicker of unease passed over her expression.

'Time to go and visit Santa, girls,' she said quickly. 'Say goodbye to the Duke.'

Despite Ciara's best efforts to get the girls to leave, Grace One refused to budge and asked, 'Prince, will you come and visit Santa with us?'

For once Tom was grateful for the endless paperwork strewn over his desk. Usually he had his administrative staff to deal with the bulk of it, preferring to conduct business either by phone or in his regular visits to his restaurants, but there was certain paperwork only he could deal with. And it frustrated the hell out of him thanks to his dyslexia.

Gesturing towards it, he said, 'Sorry, girls, but I have a lot of work to do.'

'*Please*, Prince,' pleaded Sophie.

'Santa's really nice, Prince. You can tell him what you want for Christmas,' Grace Two added passionately, her eyes alight with the magic of Christmas despite her underlying shyness.

It was going to be nigh on impossible for him to say no to their cute pleadings without coming across as a complete grouch.

'Come—it will be fun,' Ciara added. 'It will only be for ten minutes. You can get back to work after that.'

With a sigh, he stood. The three girls hopped up and down and clapped their hands. He followed Ciara and the girls out of the library, strangely moved by the girls' excitement.

In the hallway, he was taken aback when Grace One and Sophie took hold of his hands. The tiny vulnerability of their delicate fingers, the trust and innocence of their action, cracked something inside him that he struggled to name, to understand.

As a trio they followed Ciara, who was holding shy Grace's hand, along the corridor towards the main entrance hall. Along the way they met

Stephen, who frowned when he saw what was happening.

As they passed one another Tom could not resist saying, 'Nice waistcoat, Stephen.'

Today, instead of his usual formal black waistcoat, Stephen was rather self-consciously—no doubt in a nod towards Libby's instruction that they all wear fancy dress—wearing a bright red waistcoat covered in tiny green trees.

Stephen's mouth pursed.

When they had moved on a short distance Ciara turned to Tom, and they shared the connection of mischievousness that had been such a part of their teenage years.

But then Ciara looked stricken and she snapped her gaze away, as though remembering that those days of closeness were long behind them.

At the entrance hall, Ciara and Grace continued to lead the way—up the garlanded main stone staircase all the way to the second floor. Tom followed with a heavy heart, wondering just how awkward this Christmas was going to be.

To his surprise Ciara led them down the long corridor of the west wing, until they met an elf standing at the closed doorway of what had once been the family nursery.

Crouching down to be at eye level with the girls, the elf, dressed in a green tunic with red trim, green tights and pixie boots, with a green and red pixie hat balancing precariously on her head, said, 'Hi, girls. Santa is with another little girl and boy at the moment, but he said you can play in his toy workshop, if you like. It's full of special toys he thinks you will love.'

The three girls nodded enthusiastically, and when the elf stood and opened the door all three gasped.

The old nursery was unrecognisable. Converted into a North Pole toy workshop, endless fairy lights hung from its ceiling and the air was heavy with the scent of ginger and cinnamon, thanks to an enormous gingerbread house sitting on a small table at the centre of the room, with the antique dolls that had belonged to generations of Bensons surrounding it.

Against one wall sat a carpenter's bench filled with wooden carvings, where every conceivable farm animal jostled for space with toy soldiers. A gift-wrapping section sat next to the bench, its table brimming with brightly coloured presents, and a pretend production line was on the opposite side of the room, where the Benson family

Steiff teddy bears sat with quiet dignity, going round and round.

Following the elf, the girls tentatively entered the room—and then made an immediate beeline for the four-storey antique dolls' house that had often been the battlefield for many arguments between Kitty and Fran as children.

They had both coveted the bridal doll that was part of the house, and had continually argued over her. Fed up with their bickering, Tom had hidden the doll one summer, and she had only reappeared—much to everyone else's surprise—on the day they were returning to England.

Now, all these years later, Tom could finally appreciate how exquisite the dolls' house was as he stood by the girls and heard them breathlessly whispering to one another.

'Look at all the people working in the kitchen.'

'Why are they all wearing such funny dresses and hats?'

'Oh, see all the tiny furniture and the cups and saucers...and tiny glasses! And see...see the baby in her cot. There's a tiny teddy bear in with her!' raven-haired Grace called out.

Sophie added, with even more excitement, 'Look at the funny pictures of chickens.'

Tom chuckled at Sophie's description of what in fact were miniatures of a series of paintings of pheasants that hung in the formal drawing room of the castle.

Leaving the dolls' house to the girls' inspection, he found his attention grabbed by the electric train set running on the table opposite. His old train set! And all around the tracks were the vintage model pieces he had inherited from both his father and grandfather—the railway station with its nineteen-twenties tweed-dressed commuters, the wooden and redbrick signal box, the granite station water tower, the long locomotive shed...

And then he laughed, when further along the table he found his collection of toy cars. Someone had made the effort to line them all up into straight formal lines, but obviously throughout the day small hands had sent most askew. Almost instantly he found his childhood favourite—a silver Jaguar XJ220. It had started a love affair with Jaguar cars that continued up to this day.

Holding the car in his hand, the weight still so familiar, he saw the girls had now moved on from the dolls' house and were noisily arguing as to

which of the antique dolls placed at the gingerbread house table should be called Elsa.

A tightness gathered in his chest. This nursery, and Loughmore itself, had been a refuge for
him. As a young child it had given him an escape
from the constant humiliation of failing he had
endured. Now no future generations of Bensons
would ever get to play in here.

Coming to stand beside him, Ciara studied the
grey steam locomotive and green carriages as
they ran round and round the track. Her red velvet dress was cut to expose the pale skin of her
shoulders. He gazed at the delicate lines of her
collarbone, feeling a powerful urge to place his
lips there, to hold her in his arms, inhale her. It
threw him with its intensity.

He looked away, annoyed with himself. And
her. Irritation boiled in his stomach. Was all of
this—the girls' visit, their persuasion in bringing him to his childhood nursery, the ridiculously
cute outfit—all part of Ciara's scheme to stop
him selling Loughmore?

Sweeping his hand around the room, he asked,
'Whose idea was all of this?'

Ciara looked at him with a puzzled expression.
'The Duchess gave permission a few years ago

for the nursery suite to be used as a grotto. It was Libby's idea and it's been a huge hit with the children. You're unhappy about it?'

'Yes, because...'

Before he could say any more they both turned at the sound of the girls singing as they each cradled a doll and sang them a lullaby.

Their little voices filled the room.

*My heart is with you,*
*Oh, baby of mine,*
*Let the light of my love shine,*
*For ever on you.*

Ciara turned away from the girls. She was smiling. But tears shone brightly in her eyes.

He flinched, shut his eyes against the tightness enclosing his heart.

Resting both hands on the edge of the table, Ciara bowed her head as though she was studying the landscape of the model railway in great detail. Moving beside her, he placed his hand next to hers. They were almost touching. When she didn't pull away he gently placed his little finger over hers. She looked towards him. Tried to smile. But failed. Tears still glistened in her eyes.

He wanted to do more—wrap her in his arms,

whisper that he understood—but he couldn't. Not with the others in the room. And then one of the two internal doors of the nursery swung open. They shifted away from one another just as another elf appeared from what had been the nanny's sitting room.

The elf spoke to Ciara and then, turning to the girls, said 'Grace, Sophie and Grace—Santa can't wait to meet you.' Then, turning to Tom, the elf added, 'You too, Your Grace.'

Tom restrained himself from rolling his eyes.

The three girls were suddenly hit with a bout of acute shyness, and it took both Ciara and the elf to persuade them in to see Santa.

Nanny's sitting room had been transformed into Santa's Grotto, complete with giant chimney-piece and a sparkling Christmas tree. And at the centre, red-cheeked and rotund, sat a jolly Santa Claus on a red velvet throne.

'Well, if it isn't Grace Carney, Sophie O'Brien and Grace McCarthy. The three prettiest dancers I have ever seen.'

Tom bit back a smile when he recognised Liam Geary's voice coming from beneath a wildly extravagant white beard.

The three girls stared at Santa Claus, puzzled as to how he knew them.

'Now, Grace Carney, where's your brother Jack this year?' Santa asked.

Grace pouted and then shook her head with a dramatic sigh. 'He's downstairs, Santa. He said visiting you is for babies.'

'Babies?' Santa replied. 'How can it be for babies when even the Duke is visiting me?'

Grace nodded in agreement, but then leant towards Santa and said in a stage whisper, 'He's a *prince.*'

Encouraging the girls to come closer, Santa had a long chat with each of them, enquiring about school and their families, and then what it was they wanted from him this year. After promising to go to bed early the following night—Christmas Eve—the girls gave a squeal of excitement when big fat presents for each of them dropped down the giant chimney.

Santa was in the process of saying goodbye to them when Sophie interrupted him.

'What about the Prince, Santa? What will you bring him?'

'What does the Prince want?' asked Santa.

Not pausing for a beat, Tom said, 'Peace and quiet and a twenty-year-old malt.'

Santa spluttered out a laugh.

The three girls regarded him with puzzlement before Grace said determinedly, '*I* think the Prince should meet Cinderella and marry her.'

Ciara shook her head. Somebody needed to tell the girls that fairy tales simply didn't happen in real life. As if a prince would really marry a charlady from a dysfunctional family who believed that her hallucination of a rat turning into a coachman was actual reality.

Opening the door out onto the corridor, she called to the girls, 'It's time to leave, girls. I'm sure your mums will be wondering what has taken us so long. And Miss Murphy will be looking for you too.'

At the mention of Miss Murphy the three girls squealed and bolted for the door. Miss Murphy was renowned for not only being one of the best dance teachers in the country but also for her fearsomeness. She ran her dance school like a military academy.

The girls skipped down the stairs in front of Tom. She quickly followed, still embarrassed by the way she'd nearly cried in front of him. What had *that* been about? She had been enjoying the girls' reaction to the toy workshop one minute, and the next thing, when she heard their soft lullaby, she had felt as though someone had cracked her heart right open.

Inhaling a deep breath as they neared the ground floor, she knew she needed to refocus. Today was about getting Tom involved in the party—about developing an attachment in him towards Loughmore. Earlier, when he had driven her to the castle from her cottage, she had tried to persuade him to attend the party but he had refused, citing work as an excuse. She had been racking her brains for the past few hours as to how to get him involved, and then she had been gifted those three girls, who had ambushed her the moment they had arrived at the party with questions about the Prince and why he wasn't at the party.

At the bottom of the stairs the three girls ran across the marble floor, but suddenly Grace Carney came to a skating stop while the other two carried on in the direction of the ballroom. Rushing back towards Tom, she stretched her neck back to meet his eye and said, 'Prince, will you come and meet my brother Jack? He says you don't exist.'

Ciara was seriously tempted to high-five Grace Carney—she was the gift that kept on giving today. This was a great way to get Tom more involved in the party.

Before he could say no, she said quickly, 'Come along for five minutes. You can say a quick hello to Jack and everyone else there—the whole village has made a huge effort to get here today in the snow. They would appreciate you popping in.'

Tom eyed her warily. 'I need to get back to work.'

Ciara looked from Tom down to Grace. As though waiting for a signal, the moment Ciara gave her a mischievous grin Grace grabbed hold of Tom's hand and without a word began to drag him in the direction of the ballroom.

Once inside the ballroom, Grace pulled Tom over to where her twelve-year-old brother Jack was sitting at a table with his mother, scowling in the direction of the primary school *céilí* band, who were performing on the temporary stage at the top of the room.

Grace came to a dramatic stop in front of her brother and, placing her hands on her hips, said,

'Jack, this is the Prince. I *told* you he existed. See—I'm not silly.'

Jack looked in Tom's direction and folded his arms, clearly not impressed. He studied Tom before asking, 'What team do you support?'

Mimicking Jack, Tom too folded his arms and answered, 'Brighton.'

Tom's answer elicited an eye-roll from Jack even more dramatic than anything his sister was capable of producing.

Clearly flustered, Jack's mother intervened. 'Jack, *behave*! Your Grace, I'm sorry.' Standing up, she added, 'Thanks a million for hosting such a special party—it's the highlight of all the children's year.' Pausing, she looked in the direction of Jack and frowned. 'Perhaps not the pre-teens, though…you know what it's like. They can be such a handful.'

Then, stopping, she clasped a hand dramatically to her cheek.

'I should have offered my condolences. We were so sorry to hear about your father. He was a good man to the village—always willing to support us in the restoration of buildings and any charitable causes that existed. He'll be missed.'

Tom gave a tense nod.

Jack's mum regarded him with a puzzled expression, but then she said in a rush, 'Of course I'm sure you'll follow in his footsteps and be a good neighbour to the entire village.'

Tom nodded, and was in the process of backing away—no doubt in a bid to return to his work—when he was surrounded by a group of villagers who all spoke to him, offering their condolences and welcoming him back to Loughmore.

When the crowd had dispersed Ciara assumed Tom would make a dash for the door—especially as the local musical and drama group had begun a clap-along acapella version of every cheesy Christmas hit ever to have existed.

Ciara loved it. But, given Tom's pained expression, which was nothing in comparison to Jack's—who actually looked as though the singing was making his ears bleed—she guessed neither of them were particularly loving the singalong.

Tom spoke to Jack's mother, and then to Jack. Immediately Jack stood up and followed Tom out of the room, both looking as though the hounds from hell were chasing them.

When they reached the hallway, Tom said

something to Jack and Jack's scowl shifted into a beaming grin.

Ciara's smile faded. How different things could have been.

Later that evening Tom sighed when the library door swung open once again. Even before she appeared he guessed it was Ciara, because no one could swing a door open with such energy as she managed to.

Storm bounded in before her and, spotting him, charged across the floor with an enthusiasm even greater than usual and with one mighty leap jumped straight onto his lap.

Now dressed in faded blue jeans, brown suede ankle boots and an open navy and green plaid shirt over a white cotton tee shirt, Ciara propped herself against the floor-to-ceiling bookcase just inside the door. 'I suppose you can guess that Storm was missing you.'

Patting Storm, Tom asked him, 'Is Boru still terrorising you, boy?'

As if to say yes, Storm laid both of his paws on Tom's chest.

Ciara gave a guilty smile before her gaze shifted away. Her cheeks reddening, she said,

'Willy Wonka my all-time favourite movie is on TV in fifteen minutes. Will you watch it with me?'

Tom studied her for a moment. What was she up to? Pushing back his chair, he folded his arms and nodded to his phone. 'Thanks to this afternoon's diversions I'm snowed under here. I still have a mountain of phone calls to make.'

'Are you sure? Libby made some homemade chocolates… We can have some while watching it. Christmas isn't Christmas without watching some of the old classics.'

*Right.* It was time they had a frank conversation or the next few days were going to be torture.

Standing, he moved around the desk and towards her, the floorboards creaking as usual as he passed the leather club chair. 'You don't have to try to be my full-time entertainment rep, you know.'

'What do you mean?'

He settled himself beside her, one arm resting on a book shelf. 'You're not going to change my mind about selling Loughmore with your cute Christmas campaign.'

Ciara looked at him, outraged, and then huffed

and puffed for a while. He raised an eyebrow, not buying her indignation for one moment.

She stepped away from the bookcase. Folded her arms. Unfolded them. Raised them in a gesture that might be one of resignation or outrage—he couldn't quite decide.

'Okay—fine. I'll admit I won't stop trying to remind you of why you should keep Loughmore, but there was nothing orchestrated about the girls wanting to meet you. And it was their idea to ask you to visit Santa with them. Thanks for being so kind to them, by the way…' She paused and placed her hands in her back pockets, biting her lip in amusement. 'When they were leaving earlier they asked me to say goodbye to the Prince for them.'

His eyes wandered to the way the deep curve of her breasts beneath her tee shirt was revealed as her shirt shifted backwards. He was *not* going to think about how she had looked…how she had felt and tasted when they had made love all those years ago.

He looked away. Willed his pulse to calm down.

Clearing his throat, he tried to focus on what they were talking about rather than the sudden urge to reach forward and pull Ciara to him. God, what he wouldn't do to be able to wrap his arms around her waist, feel the softness of her against him once again.

'What is it with little girls and princes? What's the attraction?'

'Gosh, let me think. A good-looking, some-times decent guy who lives in a magical castle… What's there not to like?'

'*Sometimes* decent?'

'For crying out loud—you're considering sell-ing the magical castle!' Pausing, she ran her fingertips along the spines of the leather-bound books on the shelf beside her. Then, with all traces of teasing gone, she said, 'You missed the girls dancing, by the way—they were brilliant for their age. Where did you and Jack disappear to?'

'When I saw the lead singer of the musical group dragging audience members up on the stage to join in, I decided poor Jack needed rescu-ing. I took him out to the stables. He told me he's asked Santa for a pony for the past few years but has never got one—I think that's why he gives Santa such a bad rap. I let him ride Goldstar in the inside arena. He's a natural.'

'Wow, I bet you've made his Christmas.'

Her smile fading, Ciara looked away from him.

She stepped back on one foot, worrying at her lip all the while.

When she looked up again she held his gaze and then, in a soft voice close to a whisper, said, 'Jack is the same age as...'

His heart plummeted. He inhaled a shaky breath and said, 'Yes, he is.'

'Do you think...?' She paused, her mouth working.

He knew he shouldn't, but the pain, the sadness in her, had him stepping even closer. Into that space that changed everything between a man and a woman.

'Do I think about...?'

He paused too, raw fear coursing through him. It was only one word. A simple word. *Our.* But he felt he had no right to it. How would Ciara react if he used it? Had he forfeited his right to use it that day in London when he had let her down so awfully?

Clearing his throat, feeling as though he was about to step off a precipice, he said, 'Do I think about our baby?'

She blinked.

His heart banged against his chest. He was

vaguely aware of Storm head-butting his ankle, looking for a rub.

Her chest rose heavily. Then she nodded, and nodded again. Silently saying yes, that was what she wanted to know.

The urge to hold her, to tuck her forehead against the hollow of his throat, wrap himself around her and keep her safe for ever, was unbearable and also absolutely senseless.

So instead he briefly touched the pad of his thumb against her cheek and said softly, 'Yes, sometimes I do.' He stroked her arm, felt the powerful shudder that ran through her body. 'Earlier…you were upset.'

She held his gaze for a few seconds before rolling her eyes, mocking herself. 'I'm just a sentimental fool sometimes. Don't take any notice.'

Thrown by the change in her mood, he paused and considered her. This was classic Ciara. Whenever anything got too serious, too emotional, she more often than not turned it into a joke. Should he challenge her on it? Would doing so only complicate everything?

In the end he said, 'You're a lovely fool, though.'

That had her laughing. 'Wow! That's one of the nicest things anyone has ever said to me.'

'Really?

That elicited another eye-roll, but this time it was directed at him. 'No! Of course not.' She tilted her head, that rosebud mouth breaking into an intimate smile just for him. 'But it's still kind of cute.

He should step away. Go back to his work.

He knew all this but found himself saying, 'You know what? I'm tired. Let's go and watch *Willy Wonka*—I never tire of watching Augustus Gloop being sucked up the chocolate pipe.'

With a doubtful expression Ciara watched him move to the library door and open it. 'Are you sure?'

'I'm sure. But if Libby has made any rum and raisin chocolates they're all mine.'

About to pass him as he held the door open, Ciara paused, her expression put-out. 'But they're my favourite.'

With a satisfied grin he replied, 'Oh, I know that.'

Ciara shook her head, amusement glittering in her eyes. Neither of them moved. They stayed grinning at each other. And there it was again—that connection, an emotional awareness, a pull, a dangerous spark between them that had him more than worried about how he was going to survive three whole days alone with Ciara Harris.

Tearing his eyes away from those soft, glittering brown eyes, he scooped up Storm from where he was resting on his foot. 'Come on, brave fellow. It's time you stood up to that crazy cat.'

# CHAPTER FIVE

CHRISTMAS EVE...

Standing in the sunken garden to the east of the castle, watching the silver early-morning light catching the brilliance of the snow lying on the lawns running down to the lake, Ciara paused and breathed in the silence.

She loved Loughmore. She loved how difference lived in harmony here. The castle, so grand and regal, could easily dominate the estate cottages, but instead it only emphasised their small, cute perfection. The formal gardens with their polite structure were the same; their order only emphasised the wonder, the rawness, the rich natural evolution of Loughmore Wood and the Wicklow Mountains beyond.

She loved the centuries of history layering the castle so thickly you could almost touch it. She loved it all. And even though last night, as she had watched the film with Tom, his laughter had brought back so many bittersweet memories that she had been left wondering just how long she could handle being so close to him without losing her mind, standing in the garden right now reminded her of why she had to see this through and persuade him not to sell.

They had watched the movie in the Duke's Sitting Room. It was where Tom's father had retired after dinner every night and where he'd entertained close friends. Of course now it was Tom's sitting room, and it had felt awkward being in the small and intimate space with him…well, small when it came to a castle. It was at least three times the size of Ciara's own living room.

Ciara had made sure to sit in a single chair a safe distance away from where Tom had sat on the sofa, his long legs propped on a foot stool. She had thought watching a movie with him wouldn't be a big deal.

Boy, had she been wrong.

Instead of watching the movie, her eyes had kept slipping over to gaze at him. Her heart had danced at his quiet smile when Charlie had found his Golden Ticket. And then her heart had sunk when she'd stared and stared at the perfection of his neat ears, the smoothness of his forehead, the refined sharpness of his cheekbones and the nobility of that perfectly straight nose. At the strength of his neck that was matched by the broadness of his shoulders, the hard, masculine shape of his mouth that gave only the tiniest hint of how passionate and overpowering his kisses were.

Storm had lain on the sofa beside him, snoring contentedly as Tom's long, lean fingers stroked him. And she had remembered how he'd used to stroke her back after they'd made love, making her sigh with bone-deep contentment and struggle not to fall asleep under his soothing touch.

Her heart had sunk because in that moment she had admitted to herself that no other man had ever come close to Tom. She had dated other guys, trying not to compare them to him, but he had always been there. The benchmark for the knee-weakening, butterflies-in-the-stomach chemistry that drew you to a partner.

Halfway through the movie Tom had caught her staring at him. By this time—much to her dismay—a slow, torturous blaze of physical longing for him had been sweeping through her. The atmosphere in the room had instantly changed.

She had forced herself to stare at the screen,

but from the corner of her eye she'd been able to see Tom gazing in her direction.

Growing increasingly hot, she had longed for the movie to end. When it had, she'd shot out of her chair, attempted a laid-back yawn and said she'd head to bed.

She had nodded when he had gently asked if her bedroom was okay, if there was anything she needed, not trusting herself to speak in case she said, *Actually, Tom, I'd like to kiss you and have your hands on my skin. I want to feel the strength of your body pressed against mine. Frankly, I want to get all hot and bothered with you.*

He had walked with her as far as the stairs, the stillness of the castle emphasising their footsteps on the marble floor, their aloneness in the vastness of the building. She had glanced briefly in his direction and been taken aback by the tension in his expression. Then she'd muttered a goodnight and bolted up the stairs. Glad she had chosen a bedroom at the opposite side of the castle from his.

Her announcement that she was moving in to the castle for the Christmas period had been received in stunned silence when she had told the other staff. Their disquiet had dissipated, however, when she'd explained she needed to stay close to the gardens and that she would ensure the Duke was taken care of over the Christmas period even if he *was* insistent on everyone else not working for the three days.

Now, turning her back on the view, Ciara climbed up the steps at the rear of the sunken garden and stood beneath the row of Italian Cypresses that lined the raised banks. Heavy snow was starting to coat some of the branches. Raising the pole she held in her gloved hand, she stepped back as far as she could and, reaching up, knocked the worst of the snow from the first tree.

For the next while she moved along the row of trees, enjoying the satisfying thump of landing snow. Until she miscalculated the weight of snow on one tree *and* the fact that there was a Brachyglottis greyi immediately behind her, therefore blocking her ability to step out of the way of the falling snow without trampling the poor shrub.

She gasped as an avalanche headed in her direction. Snow pounded her head. Encased in white coldness, she struggled for breath. And then she yelped and screamed as snow slid down her neck and ran like an ice floe down her back.

She dropped the pole. Tugged off her jacket.

Next came her jumper. Untucking her shirt from her jeans, she did a little dance in a bid to toss out the snow that hadn't already melted.

And then she heard laughter.

Standing on the path at the other side of the sunken garden was Tom, with Storm at his side, shaking his head, clearly amused at her predicament.

He eventually managed to pull himself together enough to ask, 'Do you want any help?'

She gritted her teeth. And then called back, 'No, I'm good.'

Her response only seemed to amuse him even more. 'Now, how did I guess that you were going to insist that you're fine?'

Ciara eyed him. He was asking for it...

She pulled on her jumper and then her coat before she called over to him, 'Actually, Tom, I could use your help. There are some high-up branches I can't reach.'

Immediately he climbed down the steps of the garden. Halfway down he turned and called to Storm to follow him, but Storm ignored him in favour of sniffing at a modern metal sculpture of an Irish Red Deer.

As Tom passed the fountain in the centre of the

garden Ciara bent down and pretended to retie the lace of her work boot. When he was ten feet away she stood up.

Tom came to a stop. He narrowed his eyes, sensing danger.

From behind her back she produced a snowball. It wasn't as perfectly compact as she would have hoped. But it would do.

Quick as lightning, Tom ducked down, his hands scooping up his own heavy pile of snow.

Ciara threw her snowball. It hit him on the shoulder, snow exploding everywhere.

Shaking his hair free of the snow, Tom stood up. With a slow, disturbingly sexy grin he patted his snowball into a perfect circle.

When he threw it Ciara ducked, and gave a shout of delight when it missed her.

Tom came closer.

Unable to stop herself, Ciara gulped at the intensity of his expression. There was only going to be one winner of this snowball fight and it wasn't going to be her.

She knew she should at least stand her ground. Fight him. But seeing Tom bearing down on her, his eyes a terrifying combination of lethal amusement and purpose, she fled.

She darted in between the cypresses and out onto the path on the other side, heading towards the sanctuary of the arboretum. The path was slippery, but still she ran, thankful for her heavy-soled boots. Behind her she heard Tom curse as he slipped and skidded on the path.

She stopped and pointed out, 'You need to wear proper outdoor shoes, not brogues.'

His response was to duck down and gather more snow.

She gave another cry of satisfaction when he once again missed her.

Beneath his grey overcoat he was wearing a red jumper and dark jeans. He had a grey and white woollen hat on his head. His breath came out in puffs of steam. He looked hacked off.

He had never looked so gorgeous.

God, she was weak for him.

Tom studied the icy path and then the snow-covered lawn. Before he had even edged towards the lawn she knew what he was about to do.

She waved her hands. 'No! You can't run on the lawn. Sean will kill me...you'll damage the grass beneath. We'll be seeing your footprints for months.'

He lifted one foot over the lawn. Daring her to stop him.

'I mean it, Tom, don't walk on the grass.'

'Fine. But then you must come back here to me.'

She looked at the lawn and then at him. She'd take her chances with Sean. Twisting around, she began to run.

She could hear the soft crunch of snow behind her to her left. And it was coming closer and closer. She yelped. And then an arm was on her waist, lifting her away from the path.

They fell onto the lawn.

At first she landed on Tom, but then they were rolling as she fought him.

When they came to a stop—she on her back, Tom above her—she grabbed a fist-load of snow. But just as she was about to throw it Tom grabbed her wrist and forced her to drop it.

And then they lay there, both panting hard, their laughter fading. Unconsciously she shifted beneath him, a powerful surge of physical need engulfing her.

His eyes raked over her face. Settled on her lips.

Her heart came to a stop.

He dipped down.

Her heart spluttered as for the first time in twelve years she saw the navy flecks in his eyes. His breath mingled with hers.

She felt light-headed, dizzy with the need for him. Unconsciously she lifted her head, her lips parting.

His gaze grew darker.

A deep thrill twisted inside her.

And then his lips were on hers. Soft. Warm. Testing, as if to ask if this was what she wanted.

With shaking hands she rested her fingers on his hat, pulling him towards her.

He made a guttural sound in the base of his throat.

Every cell in her body responded with an upward surge of elation. This was so familiar—but even better than she remembered. This was everything she had missed for so many years. The finger-tingling passion of being on the receiving end of a kiss from the man you wanted to be at one with, who made your heart ache in a thousand ways.

She shifted her body again, wanting even more of his weight upon her.

His kiss became more demanding. She met him with the same hunger.

He yanked off her hat. Clasped his hands beneath her hair, his fingertips on her scalp. Deepened his kiss even more.

She cried out. Wrapped a leg around his. Lost to the brain-zinging taste of his mouth on hers.

Warmth, need and disbelief spun and spun inside her. She tightened her fingers against his skull, dizzy with the passion of his faint-inducing kiss.

But then, with a groan, Tom was pulling away, twisting his head to the side.

Storm was standing there, looking baffled by the sight of his master rolling about in the snow.

Tom dipped his head down against her throat for a second. Groaned. And then lifted himself off her. With a rueful smile he helped her stand up.

Ciara busied herself by dusting herself down. Desperate to hide the lust that must still be in her eyes given the heavy, sensual beat still pulsating in her body. Desperate to hide how disappointed she was that their kiss was over.

Tom brushed the snow off his coat too and then, studying the imprints of their bodies on the grass, he pointed and asked with a grin, 'So how are you going to explain *that* to Sean?'

Ciara groaned. She was happy to keep this light-hearted because she didn't even want to *start* to think about the implications of what had just happened between them. 'God, I don't know. Maybe I'll say a cow broke into the garden.'

Bending she swept some snow into the vacant space, praying the grass wasn't overly damaged.

Straightening, she added, 'I'd better get back to work.'

She heard the slight tremble in her voice. She was cold…but in truth it was the emptiness, the sense of loss, the confusion over their kiss that was causing her to shiver.

Tom reached for her elbow. 'What happened just now…' His voice trailed off, his expression giving nothing away.

She shrugged, desperate to get away. 'A kiss for old times' sake?'

His eyes narrowed. 'I guess…' And then with a sigh he said in a soft voice, 'There's still something between us, isn't there?'

A spectacular lump formed in her throat. His voice was so tender, so honest, so sad. She blinked back tears. 'Yes. But that doesn't mean it's right.'

He nodded at that. 'Last time we didn't say goodbye to one another the way we should have. Let's not let that happen again.'

She forced a smile. 'But we aren't going to say goodbye. I'll see you here in Loughmore whenever you come. I'll even give you a tour of my projects every time you visit, so you can see why you made the right decision in keeping Loughmore.'

Shaking his head, Tom called to Storm and, trying to hide his amusement said, 'You're incorrigible.'

Ciara watched him walk away. Alarm bells in her brain were telling her that she needed to be careful, protect herself. She needed to ensure that there were more people around. It was too dangerous when it was only the two of them.

She called after him. 'Is it okay if I invite some people over tonight for drinks?'

When he turned with a quizzical look she blushed, but forced herself to say, 'I think it would be good for us to have some company.'

He blinked as he realised what it was she was saying. With a nod, he turned away—but then turned back again. 'It was you who encouraged me to become a chef all those years ago. I think it's time I said thank you, so I'll cook Christmas dinner for us tomorrow.'

'But you're the Duke… I should be cooking for you. That's what I've planned. Libby has left me all the ingredients I need and detailed instructions.'

Tom flinched. 'When you were packing at the cottage yesterday I tested the cookies you had left out… I assume it was you who made them?'

Ciara nodded. 'And?'

'They were…*interesting*.'

Ciara could not help but laugh. 'I think you mean inedible. Okay, you make dinner. To be honest, I was dreading it.'

Once again Tom and Storm walked away.

She wanted to shout after him to get off the grass.

But God knew this was *his* castle, after all… And in a few months' time it might not matter anyway if Tom was serious about selling.

Which would mean she would never see him again.

He turned when he reached the steps, gave a slight nod before he disappeared from view.

She swallowed against the tight lump in her throat. Then took her phone out of her jacket pocket and began to phone her friends who lived nearby to invite them over for drinks.

Popping open a bottle of champagne that evening, Tom filled the glasses of all those present—Liam Geary and his wife Maeve, Libby, Vince McNamara and Ciara—before proposing a toast, 'Wishing you all a happy and peaceful Christmas.'

Everyone dutifully tapped their glasses, but there was an awkwardness in the room. Liam kept fingering his collar while Maeve looked decidedly pale...especially in comparison to Libby, who looked as though she was seriously overheating.

Only Vince seemed immune to the unease. He had swept into the room a little earlier in the company of Libby, gasping loudly at his surroundings before enthusiastically complimenting the décor.

The drawing room had always been Tom's favourite room in Loughmore, but it still surprised him just how proud he had felt at Vince's admiration for the thirty-foot-long room, with its ornate gilded ceiling, rich red tapestry rugs, the two

Christmas trees flanking the marble fireplace, the red and gold thread curtains and the antique side tables and sofas commissioned by the Sixth Duke of Bainsworth in Paris.

Toast over, they all stood at the centre of the room, Libby, Liam and Maeve avoiding eye contact with him.

An uneasy silence fell, until Ciara intervened by saying, 'I mentioned to you that Vince's husband Danny is away skiing? Unfortunately he didn't make it back to Loughmore before the snowstorm… It was to be their first Christmas together.'

Tom turned to Vince. 'I'm sorry to hear that.'

Vince gave an unconvincing shrug of bravado before putting his arm around Libby's shoulders, 'I may not have Danny tomorrow, but I do have Libby—we're spending the day together. And as for Danny—he's in Dublin being spoilt rotten by his mother as we speak.'

Tom smiled at the affection in Vince's eyes when he said Danny's name.

Maeve obviously saw it too, because she said in a voice full of warmth, 'Marriage suits you, Vince. I don't think I've ever seen you so happy.'

Vince batted his hand and grew a little red

while tears formed in his eyes. He nodded, and then with a laugh admitted, 'It *is* wonderful...to find someone you love so much and who loves you back with equal passion... I never knew I could feel so loved, so secure. What more would you want in life?'

Liam and Maeve nodded in agreement before sharing a private look.

Tom twisted the stem of his champagne glass and willed himself not to glance in Ciara's direction. But that lasted all of five seconds. He looked over at her. She met his gaze before dipping her head, a small blush forming on her cheeks.

His heart punched hard against his ribs. Why had he kissed her this morning? Why was he complicating things when he had sworn to himself he wouldn't? He had said they'd be friends. Friends didn't kiss. And certainly not the kind of hot, lustful, memory-provoking kiss they had shared this morning. Why was he leaving himself open to the pain and bewilderment of twelve years ago all over again?

But the worst part of it all was that he should bitterly regret the kiss, but he didn't. How could he when it had been so glorious, so intimate, so beautiful. Kissing Ciara was like nothing else.

It sent his senses crazy but it also gave him an emotional warmth, a sense of belonging, a sense of being true to himself that was as wonderful as it was bewildering.

Libby broke the silence in the room. 'Right. That's my New Year resolution sorted out. I'm going back to online dating. There has to be someone out there for me. You too, Ciara... Let's be dating partners.'

Ciara. Dating. Hundreds of men staring at her profile picture. No way.

He turned to Libby. 'Online dating can be dodgy.'

Libby gave him a doubtful look. 'I suppose...'

Libby looked so crestfallen, and so nervous of him once again, that he gave her a smile and said, 'I have a number of guys working in my restaurants who are single. I can introduce them to you...you'd share the same passion for cooking.'

Libby looked startled at first by his suggestion, but then her face lit up. 'Wow...if you wouldn't mind.' Pausing, she gave a little laugh. 'I didn't think you would be a matchmaker, Your Grace. Sounds like our love lives might be improving next year, Ciara!'

Ciara gave Libby a dubious look. 'Perhaps...'

Then, looking around the group, she said with a little too much enthusiasm, 'Why don't we play a party game?'

Tom could not help but moan.

Liam laughed and said, 'I'm with you, Your Grace.'

Tom threw his eyes to heaven. 'For crying out loud, people—stop calling me that. I'm *Tom*.'

They all nodded, and the tension in the room eased even further as their nods were joined with broad smiles of relief.

He spoke to the group, but to Liam and Libby in particular. 'I may be the Duke, but I see all our roles as being of equal value and importance. I know in the past my father kept everything very formal, but that's not my style. I run my restaurants on the basis of trust and respect, with everyone from the waiting staff up to my executive chefs treated with the same value. I want the same with my estates.'

Vince raised his glass and said, 'Hear, Hear.'

They all good-naturedly tapped their glasses again.

Then Vince added, 'Now, can we get on with a party game? I propose charades.' Wrapping his arms around Libby's and Ciara's waists, he drew them to the stuffed velvet sofa at one side of the fireplace, 'Libby and Ciara—you'll be on my team.' When all three had settled on the sofa, Vince said with a cheeky grin, 'Tom, Liam and Maeve—you can be on the losing team.'

Liam exchanged a look with him. It was game on.

Ciara was the first up. The two groups had spent some time coming up with suitable titles for the opposing teams, which they had typed into the memo section of their phones.

Ciara read the title on Liam's phone screen. Her eyes twinkled and she hit him with a much too self-satisfied grin. 'That's easy.'

Maeve threw a dirty stare towards Liam, who was sitting beside her on the sofa. 'I told you it was too easy.'

Ciara turned to her group.

Vince enthusiastically responded to her gestures. 'It's a book. Four words. The third word is *the*.'

Libby joined in, 'The second word is small… An…is…it…to…'

Ciara shook her head.

'Of!' Vince shouted.

Ciara gave a thumbs-up.

'Fourth word…'

Libby and Vince stared at Ciara as she moved up and down the floor, flapping her arms at her sides.

'Bird. A penguin. A crow.'

'A robin. A thrush. A chicken.'

'An ostrich!' Libby shouted.

For some reason this cracked Ciara up. She shook her head, tears of laughter bubbling in her eyes. She tried to do her acting out again but kept stopping, overcome with laughter.

The gold sequinned dress she was wearing stopped at mid-thigh. Her legs seemed to go on for ever until they reached the pale gold stiletto shoes on her feet. Her hair was tied up in a loose chignon. She looked absolutely beautiful, standing before the fireplace, the sequins in her dress flashing as they caught the lights from the Christmas trees and the flames from the fire… And Tom realised in that moment that it would be so easy to fall in love with her all over again.

He flinched at the idea. Ciara would never love him back. How could she after all the pain he had caused her?

In their time together they had never uttered the words *I love you*—perhaps both of them had known they were too young for such a momentous statement, too scared of the implications.

Her teasing, her batting away of his compliments, had eased, though, in the weeks before they had made love—and in the weeks that had followed. She had softened, had listened to him with an intensity that had cracked open his heart. And she had walked straight in. Their love for one another had been there in their lovemaking. In the way she had gazed into his eyes with an unwavering honesty, vulnerability, trust.

A trust he had destroyed.

Now, across the room, Libby and Vince were shouting out every bird name they could think of, totally ignoring Ciara's hand-waving as she tried to silently tell them they had gone down the wrong track with their obsession with bird names.

Throwing her hands up in the air, she eventually caught their attention by pushing her right index finger forward.

'First word,' Vince said.

Ciara pointed back to Tom.

He could not help but smile at the seriousness of her expression. She was determined to win.

'Tom… Your Grace…' Vince called out.

Ciara nodded, but then shook one hand from side to side, to indicate that it was something similar.

With pleasure, Tom called out, 'You only have fifteen seconds left.'

That started an avalanche of answers from Vince. 'Duchess… Queen… Boss… King.'

'King of the Jungle!' Libby called.

'King of the Castle!' Vince shouted.

By now Ciara was once again shaking with laughter.

'Time is up,' Tom announced.

Libby and Vince groaned.

Ciara threw her hands up in the air, and with laughter bubbling in her voice said to her team-mates, 'It was *Lord of the Flies*, you twits.'

Later, after seeing the others to the door, Tom found Ciara in the kitchen. She gave him a quick smile before placing the now empty bottles of champagne into the glass recycling bin. Then she began to fill the dishwasher with the cups and saucers they had used.

She gave a chuckle. 'Libby looked as though

she was going to pass out when you insisted on making tea and coffee for everyone.' Then, after a pause, she added, 'It was a fun night. Did you enjoy it?'

There was tentativeness in her question.

He eyed her, pretending to think deeply.

She straightened, a cup still in her hand. Waiting for him to answer.

Eventually he answered with a grin, 'It was fun. Especially beating you at charades.'

She scowled at him, but then laughed.

A happiness, a contentment, spread through him like warming brandy. God, he loved being able to make her smile.

Her eyes moved beyond him, and he turned and saw she was looking towards the kitchen clock.

In a low, eager voice she said, 'It's only half an hour until midnight. Right now is my all-time favourite time of year. Don't you think there's something magical in the air?' She paused and tilted her head. 'I always think that if I listen hard enough I might hear Santa's sleigh.'

'Just how much champagne did you have?'

She glared at him light-heartedly. 'My own Christmas grouch!'

She had called him a grouch. He should be put out. But instead a deep pleasure fizzed through him. *My own…* She had said those words with such warmth.

Taking the cup from her, he placed it in the dishwasher. Then, shutting the door, he said, 'Let's go greet Santa.'

He told her to change into something warmer, and to wear outdoor shoes, and then turned away when she bounded up the stairs, her short skirt bringing back the memory of her leg curling around his earlier that morning. He had burned with the desire to yank off her coat…to lift her jumper and feel the soft skin of her stomach. To place his lips there and then move upwards to the sweet swell of her breasts.

Within five minutes she was racing back down the stairs, zipping up a padded jacket.

He took her outside and they followed the path down to the lake. At the lake house he pulled out two of the wicker garden chairs stored there for summer picnics on the lake and a couple of blankets. Positioning them on the wooden jetty, he told Ciara to sit on one, passed her a blanket and, after switching off the lake house light, joined her.

It was a brilliantly clear night. Millions of stars hung over them and the moon was a gentle crescent.

Sitting, he said into the still night, 'I reckon this is the best place to see Santa.'

Her laughter rippled out along the lake. 'I take it all back—maybe you're not a grouch after all.'

For the past couple of days he had thought her enthusiasm for Christmas was based on her campaign to stop him selling Loughmore. But now he realised it was genuine.

'Why do you love Christmas so much?'

She shifted in her seat, pulling the blanket more tightly around herself. She tilted her head back and stared at the stars for a while before answering. 'When I was growing up, as you know, it was just myself and my mum. We had no other family to spend Christmas with and it was all a little sad, to be honest. We used to eat Christmas dinner in front of the TV. My mum wasn't into decorating the house too much. It was nothing like the fun family celebrations I saw in the movies. My memories of Christmas are all a little grey... I guess I'm trying to make up for that now.'

Adjusting her hat with gloved fingers, she pulled it down too far, the brim covering her eyes. She giggled to herself. Lifting the brim, she caught his gaze. His heart stumbled at the warmth, the hope, the excitement in her eyes.

'Christmas should be joyful. It should be a time you spend with people you love.' She stopped abruptly, looking at him wide-eyed. 'Like to-night—I love Vince and Libby to bits. They're good friends. And Liam and Maeve have been really supportive since I came to Loughmore. Their sons live abroad, in Vancouver and Perth. They miss them greatly—I think Maeve likes to mother me in their absence.'

She gave him a quick smile. Flustered.

'So—what was Christmas like in the Benson family?'

'Noisy. Chaotic. My parents always had friends and family to come and stay for the Christmas period. As you would have seen by the large number of guests who came here to Loughmore during your summer stays, my parents liked to entertain.'

'You didn't like them entertaining?'

'It always felt like we children were lost amongst all those guests. Now, with hindsight,

I can see it was my father's way of ignoring all the things that were wrong in his life.'

'Like what?'

'His marriage. The financial strain running such a vast estate brings. My father was deeply ambitious and driven. He felt he had to live up to the title of Duke—be superhuman somehow, larger than life. All his achievements—socialising, entertaining, his obsession for polo—were how he thought a duke should behave. He was an overly proud man, who would never ask for help from anyone. And he didn't accept weakness in others.'

'And you were caught up in all that?'

'Fran, Kitty and I spent very little time with our parents. As you know, we were sent to boarding school from the age of seven, and when we were at home the houses were always full of visitors that had to be entertained.'

'I often wondered about your mum—didn't she miss you when you left home at such a young age?'

His mother had been a remote figure when he was growing up. He had felt as though all her energy had been consumed in keeping his father happy. No wonder he had fallen so hard for

Ciara—elated to finally have someone so gregarious and giving in his life.

'My father had such a big and powerful personality, it dominated their marriage. I know she loved him, but it was as though she was constantly trying to please him, placate him. She's changed since my father died. Since he's gone she's more relaxed. When he was alive we had a difficult relationship. She always took his side.'

'Against you?'

'He threatened me with disinheritance when I became an apprentice chef. My mother stood by his stance.'

Ciara sat forward in her chair. Touched her hand against his knee. Settled her troubled eyes on him. 'Tom, why didn't you tell me?'

*Because I knew you would worry, feel responsible for encouraging me to follow my dreams. I wanted to protect you, Ciara. I wanted to make you proud. I was sick of feeling like a failure.*

He didn't say any of those things to her. Instead he held her gaze and thought of his mother, and how she had spent her lifetime trying to win his father's love. 'My mother was never certain of my father's love. It's almost destroyed her.'

Ciara's hand remained on his knee. Over the

treetops and along the flat calm surface of the lake skimmed the sound of church bells.

Ciara blinked. Said in a whisper, 'It's Christmas Day.' She swallowed. Tears shone in her eyes. 'Happy Christmas, Tom.'

The weight of her hand on his knee, her nearness, her soft compassion, the care in her eyes, almost undid him.

For a brief second she closed her eyes, and then added in another whisper, 'I thought of you every Christmas—wondered how you were.'

That hit him like a boot in the stomach. He wanted to shout at her not to say things like that. He wanted to drag her on to his lap, wrap his arms about her and lose every part of himself in her.

Instead he nodded and quietly spoke the truth. 'I thought about you too.'

Ciara sighed heavily. A sigh full of sadness and regret, but a sigh that also said that it was all in the past. And she was right. They needed to move on.

So, despite the urge to pull her into him, to feel her lips beneath his again, he stood and said as light-heartedly as he could, 'Right, you need to go to bed, Ciara Harris, or Santa won't come and leave you any presents.'

# CHAPTER SIX

THE FOLLOWING MORNING, about to enter the breakfast room, Ciara stumbled to a stop—thanks to the sight of Tom strolling towards her with that easy, sexy saunter that had always been her undoing as a teenager.

Her knees wobbled, threatening to give way, and it had nothing to do with the weight of the tray she was carrying. Yep, that saunter still managed to nail her.

His hair damp, today he was wearing slim-fitting navy trousers and a pale blue shirt, the top button undone.

Early Christmas morning and Tom Benson.

A lethal combination of pleasure and potential disaster.

Images raced through her mind—Tom in the shower just now, earlier asleep in his bed… They had only ever managed to spend one whole night together, but the image of him curled into her, the long length of his eyelashes fluttering when he muttered in his sleep, his arm lying heavily on her waist, was deeply ingrained in her memory. She had lain there as the sun had peeled away the night, astonished and scared that she could feel so much for another person.

Now she held her breath as his eyes moved over her, taking in her cream blouse with its wide bow at the neck, her black cigarette pants. She was pointlessly pleased by the attraction in his eyes.

His eyebrows flickered upwards when his gaze settled on her bare feet, her toenails painted bright scarlet in honour of the season.

She gave him an apologetic smile. Despite the fact she had only been wearing her black patent stilettos for little more than an hour, her feet had ached in them so badly she had jettisoned them earlier, while working in the kitchen.

It was a good job Stephen wasn't around—he would have a conniption if he found her wandering around the castle shoeless. Especially as the bluebell tattoo on her right foot was visible.

A surge of embarrassment ripped through her as she remembered the various other social faux pas she had unwittingly committed as a teenager when around the Benson family. Kitty and Fran had always responded with giggles, while Tom's mother would look away with an expression that suggested she was yet again disappointed in the whole of mankind. His father would simply glare in her direction, as though wondering who'd allowed this simpleton into his household.

As Tom neared her, she tried to shake off all those thoughts. 'Good morning. Breakfast is ready. If you would like to take a seat, I'll go and fetch some tea for you.'

Tom regarded her curiously. Then, glancing into the breakfast room, he asked, 'Why is the table only set for one?'

Last night, as she had tossed and turned in bed, remembering their kiss on the lawn that morning, and the searing heat that had consumed her despite the ice-cold snow beneath her, remembering the affection in Tom's eyes later as she had failed hopelessly at her turn in charades, the pull she'd felt towards him as they had sat by the lake awaiting Christmas Day, she had known she needed to back off, to be more careful around him. She was once again losing herself to him. Forgetting all the reasons why they could never be together.

'I...well...staff don't normally eat with the family.'

With clear impatience he took the tray from her and entered the room. 'Come on, Ciara, you're more than staff.' Depositing the tray on the table, he turned to her and said, 'I thought we were friends.'

She followed him into the room. Placed her hands on the back of one of the twelve carved walnut chairs surrounding the breakfast table. 'It's all getting a little messy.'

Tom folded his arms. 'I'm sorry about our kiss yesterday.'

Despite herself, she flinched. Unable to look at him, she moved her gaze to the bay window of the room. It was snowing again beyond the sash window.

Behind her the fire snapped and hissed gently.

'What time were you up this morning?'

She turned at his impatient question. 'Just after seven.' When his expression hardened she added, 'I couldn't sleep. Rather than lie there I thought I would get your breakfast ready.'

'I don't expect you to look after me, Ciara.'

How was she going to explain that she felt safer when their roles were clearly defined? When there were boundaries set down by centuries of tradition that dictated staff were never even to *attempt* to mix with the family, to believe they were equals.

Going to the tray, she lifted off a silver pot of marmalade and a silver jug filled with milk. Trying not to blurt out the crazy thoughts rampaging through her mind.

*Maybe I want to look after you, Tom. Not in the way a staff member takes care of her boss. But in the way a couple look out for one another. Do something nice to make your day pleasurable.*

'I'll go and get you some tea…or would you prefer coffee?'

'For crying out loud…'

With that Tom left the room. Ciara chased after him. He was heading in the direction of the kitchen.

Once in the kitchen, he slammed the kettle onto the heating plate of the range. And then he turned to her. 'You're joining me for breakfast. Tea or coffee?'

Ciara hesitated, but then she saw the tiniest hint of amusement tugging at Tom's mouth. Her own mouth twitched. She folded her arms and gave him her best evil look. 'You were always bossy, Tom Benson.'

'And *you* were always useless at keeping a straight face.'

With a feeling of ridiculous pride, Ciara watched Tom finish his breakfast of smoked salmon and scrambled eggs on soda bread. Outside, snow still gently floated past the bay window. The fire continued to crackle, heating the room with a soothing warmth that induced the need for a quick nap—as evidenced by Storm, who was laid out before the hearth, snoring contentedly.

Tom chuckled as Storm gave a particularly loud snuffle.

Ciara felt a dizzying, out-of-body disorientation. What was she, a working-class girl from Dublin, doing sitting in the breakfast room of Loughmore Castle on Christmas Morning, having breakfast with the Eleventh Duke of Bainsworth?

She sipped her tea. Meeting Tom's eye over the rim of her cup. His smile faded. To be replaced by an intensity that matched the violent sweep of attraction hijacking her own body.

Her heart rolled in her chest.

Springing out of her chair, she began to clear the table. Needing to be busy. Needing to ignore the ever-increasing simmering tension between them.

She gave her best cheerful grin, and hoped her voice sounded breezy. Back in entertainment rep mode, to use Tom's words. 'After I clear up, let's open our presents under the tree.'

Standing too, Tom began to clear away the dishes, saying nothing.

His silence unsettled her. Only adding to her feeling of jitteriness.

She had known being alone with him, spending so much time together, would be difficult. But she hadn't expected to be so physically drawn to him, so crazily craving to be in his company. She actually missed him when they were apart. What madness was taking her over?

She lifted the tray she had loaded. Almost buckled under its weight. She had absentmindedly overloaded it.

Taking it from her, Tom placed it back onto the table. Lightly he placed his hands on her shoulders and held her gaze. 'Breathe, Ciara…relax.'

What did he mean? She gave him a puzzled look. And then, seeing the amusement in his eyes, she laughed out loud at her ability to freak herself out so easily.

Her laughter shifted the tension in the room and together they cleared the table and cleaned up in the kitchen, with Tom telling her about his restaurants, making her giggle by recounting humorous incidents with customers.

When they'd finished they moved to the drawing room. Tom shook his head as his gaze took in the already lit fire, the twinkling lights of the two trees flanking the fireplace and the pile of Christmas presents she had earlier placed beneath one of the trees. 'There was no need…'

She shushed him by kneeling down on the rug beneath one of the trees and pushing a pile of brightly wrapped presents towards him. 'These are all yours.'

Taken aback, he stared at them. 'From whom?'

'The small rectangular present in the silver paper is from the staff here in Loughmore and the others are from me and Boru.'

He sat down on a nearby chair and studied the pile. His gaze travelled back to her. The smile he gave her warmed every cell in her body.

'Thank you.' Then, running a hand over the

smooth skin of his jawline, he said ruefully, 'Let me guess—Boru has given me anti-scratch ointment.'

'No. But, you know, that's not a bad idea for next year.'

Too late she realised what she had said. There would be no 'next year'. This Christmas was going to be a one-off.

She forced down the dismay that came with that thought and nodded to his pile. 'Come on—aren't you going to open them?'

He selected the rectangular present wrapped in shiny red paper first. He opened it up, studied it and then turned the photo frame towards her. It was a photo of the castle she had taken early yesterday morning. With the grounds blanketed in snow, the castle had never looked so magical. She had driven into the village yesterday afternoon to print the photo at Murphy's Chemists, and also to pick up some other presents for Tom.

Tom gave her a dubious look. 'It's a stunning photo…but certainly not the most subtle present I have ever received.'

She feigned innocence. 'It's not often we have snow in Ireland. I thought you'd appreciate a me-

mento to have with you when you're not here in Loughmore.'

He raised his eyes heavenwards, not buying it for a moment. Then nodding towards her pile he said, 'Your turn.'

She selected a square present wrapped in paper bearing images of hundreds of tiny jolly Santas riding their sleighs through the night sky. Libby had given it to her. Ripping the paper open, she laughed at the present inside. 'A board game based on Truth or Dare. Libby knows of my addiction to board games.'

When Tom opened his next present he sighed deeply and once again turned it around towards her. 'Really?'

A few years ago, when Tom had announced he was opening a restaurant in Paris, a renowned Parisian restaurateur had been scathing about Tom's, calling the food 'pedestrian.' Tom had stayed silent on the criticism, but a year later, after Tom's, Paris, had received a host of food awards, he had invited the other restaurateur for dinner at Tom's during a radio interview. The restaurateur was yet to take up the invitation.

Trying to keep a straight face, Ciara held out her hand for the cookbook by that restaurateur, intending to pretend to flick through the recipes. 'I thought you should keep up to date with what your competition are doing.'

Tom passed the book to her, but when she took hold of it refused to let go. 'So you've been keeping an eye on my career?'

Ciara willed herself not to blush. She pulled at the book, but still Tom would not let go. He was clearly not going to give in until she gave a response.

'Call it a passing interest.'

He laughed. Clearly not buying that either.

She ignored how pleased he looked at the fact that her teasing present to him had backfired, with her now being the one embarrassed, and grabbed another of her presents.

This one was from Maeve and Liam. It was a bottle of perfume. One she had not used before. Opening the package, she admired the ornate flower-shaped bottle top and sprayed some of the perfume on her wrists and throat. She was enveloped by a light but sensual floral scent that reminded her of sweet peas in August, with a backdrop of delicate lemon.

Then, unconsciously, she leaned towards Tom and held her wrist out. 'Isn't this incredible?'

Tom leant over her wrist. The tip of his nose touched her skin. A deep craving so hot and lusty that it threatened to split her in two shot down through the centre of her body.

For a brief moment he took hold of her wrist. She swayed at his light grasp. Then, lowering her hand, he said in a low voice that held a dangerous note, 'You should wear it all the time.'

*All the time…* Including in bed? She shook off that thought and lifted another of his presents. Trying to be light-hearted, she waved it about. 'Bet you can't guess what this is!'

'Let me see… A cylindrical box with something moving inside it. Tennis balls for Storm to chase? A map for buried treasure?'

Lifting another small present, Ciara showed it to him. 'Storm has his own present to open. And you certainly don't need a map for buried treasure.'

'I wouldn't be so sure of that.'

Ciara looked at him curiously but he shrugged away his words.

Calling to Storm, who was half hidden under the sofa behind Ciara, dozing once again, Tom laughed when he opened Storm's present to reveal a red and green chequered neckerchief. Placing it around Storm's collar, Tom rubbed him vigorously before opening the cylindrical box.

'Twenty-year-old malt whiskey...there was no need.'

Ciara sliced her hand through the air, silencing him. 'You asked Santa for it—of course there was a need.'

He laughed. 'I also remember asking for peace and quiet.'

'That will come...once you decide to keep Loughmore.'

Tom looked down at Storm, shaking his head. 'She gives with one hand...takes with the other.'

Ciara had one final box to open. It was a huge present wrapped in gold paper from Vince and Danny. Last night when Vince had given it to her she had tried refusing to accept it, instinctively knowing, even without opening it, that it would be a much too generous gift. But Vince had insisted she accept it, explaining that it was his and Danny's way of thanking her for looking after their menagerie of pets when they were away on honeymoon earlier in the year.

Ciara opened the box with her breath held tight. Beneath a thick layer of gold tissue paper was a white and gold strapless gown. She gasped when she pulled it out. Standing, she held it against herself, her hands flaring over the full skirt that reached to her mid-calf. It was the most stunning piece of clothing she had ever seen.

'Danny is a buyer for one of the major department stores in Dublin. He was showing me some of the winter collection online one night and I fell in love with this. It was out of stock at the time. I can't believe he found it for me.'

Her heart came to a stop when she looked back at Tom. He was studying the dress hard and then he stared at her. His voice was deep, possessive, when he spoke. 'You will look amazing wearing it.'

She laughed off his compliment. 'I need to find somewhere to wear it first.'

His gaze shifted away from her. He rolled his shoulders. Eventually he said, 'Come to the New Year's Eve ball.'

Ciara clutched the dress tighter to herself. Why had he hesitated before asking her? And, anyway, was he even being serious? Staff *never* went to the ball. Nor did any of the locals. The Loughmore New Year's Eve ball was attended by the rich and famous and titled. 'I can't.'

'Why not?'

'I'd only embarrass you—like that time at your eighteenth birthday party, when I said I hated a particular movie only to find out the producer was actually sitting at the table, listening to my every word. I thought your father was going to kill me.'

Tom tried his best not to laugh. 'It *was* an awful movie.' Then, his expression sobering, he asked, 'Will you come?'

For a moment she considered pointing out all the reasons why she couldn't but, not wanting to destroy the Christmas atmosphere, she said instead, 'I'll think about it.'

Kneeling down again, she passed his last present to him and began to fold away her dress.

Unwrapping the metallic silver paper, Tom opened the ruby-red presentation box inside. Lifting out a heavy metal key, he weighed it in his hands before saying in a low voice, 'The key to Loughmore.'

'Apparently it's tradition for the staff to give every new Duke a key,' Ciara explained.

Tom inhaled deeply and studied her with a perplexed expression. 'Didn't you try to stop this? You *know* what my intentions are.'

'And you know I don't agree with them.'

With that Tom stood and, grabbing all the paper strewn on the floor, crumpled it all into a tight ball. 'I'll go and make dinner.'

Standing too, Ciara faced him, fear at the thought of Loughmore falling into developers' hands having her say sharply, 'Tell me why you have to sell Loughmore, Tom? I still don't understand.'

He let out an angry breath, his nostrils flaring. He turned to walk away but then swung round. 'My father has left the estate in debt. I have no option.'

Dumbfounded, she stared at him. 'Tom… I'm sorry. I had no idea.'

He shook his head impatiently and turned away again.

She followed him instantly and reached for his arm. 'This must be a huge worry for you.'

He slowly turned to her, the frustration in his expression giving way to a guarded tiredness.

Blushing, she shook her head, frustrated and annoyed with herself, 'And there I was, giving you a hard time. I wasn't exactly being any help, was I?'

Tom threw the ball of wrapping paper onto the chair behind him. 'You weren't to know.'

'Would you keep Loughmore if the finances allowed it?'

'Maybe.'

'I thought your restaurants…?'

He raked a hand through his hair. 'I don't want to burden my restaurant business with the debts of the estate. They're two separate entities.'

'Is there anything I can do?'

His jaw tightened. 'There's nothing *anyone* can do.' But then his irritation seemed to melt away and with a faint smile he admitted, 'But you asking that means a lot to me.'

Her heart skipped at the sincerity in his voice.

'As do all the presents…' He paused. 'I almost forgot *your* present. Wait here—I'll go fetch it from my office.'

Though Ciara hadn't expected a present from him, she could not help but be secretly chuffed that he had thought to give her one, and when he came back into the room carrying a small package she tried to keep a lid on her excitement.

Opening the glittering snowflake-printed paper, she felt a solid lump form in her throat. Inside the wrapping was the antique Irish wildflower identification book she had spent so many summers poring over in the Loughmore library when no one else had been about.

She held the book out to Tom. 'I can't… I can't accept this. It's too rare—too valuable.'

Tom backed away. 'It's yours. To the rest of us it's just another book amongst the thousands lining the shelves of the library. I know how much you used to love it and I want you to have it.'

Ciara's throat closed over. She did love this book. Opening it, she turned the pages. The full-page illustrations of wildflowers such as bog myrtle and Marsh-marigold on heavyweight paper, with interlining tissue guards to protect them, were as intricate and vibrant as she remembered. But what was getting to her even more was the fact that Tom had remembered her love for it.

'Now, I guess I'd better go and make that dinner I promised you.'

She looked up at Tom's words. 'I'll help.'

He looked as though he was about to argue with her, so before he could she intercepted him. 'I'd enjoy watching you cook.'

A wicked grin formed on his mouth and Ciara tried not to blush. That had sounded all wrong.

Eventually, after grinning at her for much too

long, he put her out of her misery by saying, 'Okay, but you're on veg prep.'

Together they walked to the kitchen, with Storm loudly giving chase to Boru when he spotted him slinking into the Billiard Room. Ciara's heart sang to hear Tom's laughter when both animals bounded out of the room, Storm slipping and sliding on the marble floors as he tried to capture his arch nemesis.

Later that evening, Ciara wobbled on her high heels, fully understanding now why Storm struggled so much on the smooth marble floors of Loughmore. Stopping at the entrance to the dining room, she tugged on the bottom of her dress, questioning once again if she had made the wrong choice in what to wear for dinner.

It was embarrassing enough that she had looked blankly at Tom when he'd earlier suggested they change for dinner. It had taken her a few minutes to realise he meant they should dress up for the occasion…well, dress up more than they already were.

Given that she spent the majority of her days outdoors, she didn't have many dressy outfits in her wardrobe, and as she had already worn two of her limited supply in recent days she had spent the last half an hour agonising over whether the high street dress she had purchased for the nightclubs of Ibiza when she had gone there on holidays two summers ago was suitable for Christmas dinner with a duke in his fairy tale castle.

*No*, was probably the correct answer to that question.

Entering the candlelit room, she willed herself to remain calm when Tom stood up from his seat at the top of the table. Dressed in a dark navy suit, white shirt and a navy tie with small red polka dots, gold cufflinks glittering in the candlelight, he looked completely at home in his opulent surroundings. His gaze slid down her body, his expression darkening, and Ciara's heart kicked wildly in her chest.

When she neared him he held out the chair to his right for her to sit on. Maggie and Stephen had set the table before they'd left for their break with their usual meticulousness. A huge centrepiece of fresh red roses scaled to accommodate the vastness of the twenty-two-seater table sat in the middle, with four tall candelabra on either side. A smaller version of the centrepiece sat between her and Tom.

They had spent hours in the kitchen together, with Tom patiently explaining what he was doing and how she could help and the radio playing Christmas songs in the background. Even though she had been hyper-aware of him, the mood had been relaxed as they'd worked together. But now all that had changed. Was it the dimness of the room? The act of eating dinner alone? The fact that her dress was probably a tad too short?

Then, as she was about to take the proffered seat, her attempt at calmness became a distant memory when he bent and kissed her cheek. His lips were warm…tingle-inducingly firm. She breathed in citrus and leatherwood. Her hand reached for his arm to steady herself. But the strength, the hard muscle she found there, only made her feel even more breathless.

His lips lingered for long seconds. And then he murmured, 'Happy Christmas, Ciara.'

Her head swam.

Tom stepped back, his gaze moving over her once again. 'Please tell me you've never worn that dress out in public.'

His voice was unsettlingly husky. She tried to ignore the melting sensation in her bones.

Placing a hand on the Balmain-inspired brown and black sequin-embellished dress she shrugged innocently. 'I've only worn it to the County Wicklow Gardening Awards ceremony.'

Tom's jaw stiffened. 'You aren't being serious?'

She let him dangle for a few seconds before giving a laugh. 'Of *course* I'm not being serious! I might not be the best with social etiquette, but even *I* know this is a bit much for an event where the average age is sixty-five.'

Taking her seat, she accepted the white wine Tom offered her before he went over and took their starters from the warming oven in the adjacent Dinner Service Room.

She gripped the stem of her wine glass, fighting the compulsion to tell him to sit down—that it was she who should be serving him. And when he sat beside her, so at ease, born to be surrounded by such beauty and luxury, she felt like a complete fraud.

She did not belong here.

She bit her lip.

Tom's gaze narrowed. 'Is something the matter?'

She shook her head, too embarrassed to try to

explain how out of place she felt. And also determined not to ruin their first…and only… Christmas meal together.

She tried to keep her sighs to a minimum as she hungrily ate the velvety and luscious cauliflower velouté with black truffle, but one eye-roll of pure pleasure too many had Tom grinning from ear to ear.

For their main course Tom had cooked a fillet of cod with a poached egg on a bed of crushed potatoes, with beurre blanc and roasted root vegetables.

Taking a mouthful of the delicate fish, she felt her eyes twitch with the need to close them in delight.

Biting back a smile at Tom's expectant look in her direction, she shook her head sadly. 'It's not turkey—I always have turkey on Christmas Day.'

He stabbed at his potatoes with a fork. 'So you've been reminding me—all afternoon.'

She bit back a smile. 'It's… It's…' She paused, his eyes narrowed, and tilted her head. 'It's the most fantastic dish I have ever tasted.'

Later that evening Tom reluctantly allowed Ciara drag him into the drawing room. Before the fire she had placed a large upholstered ottoman that was groaning under the weight of various board games.

Slipping off her shoes, she knelt before the ottoman. 'Indulge me for an hour.'

In her kneeling position, even more tantalising inches of her toned legs were exposed. He knew he was staring, so he forced his gaze away, and then he was captured by the beauty of the fiery depths of her hair glistening in the firelight, the seductive shimmering of the sequins of her dress. But it was her eyes, bright and gleaming, that captured his heart.

A ton of worry lodged in his chest. He was growing too close to her. Letting her into his heart. Earlier, when he had told her about the estate's debts, her empathy had broken through the burden he had been carrying around for the past few months. And later, as they had prepared dinner together, they had worked in easy companionship. Ciara, despite her teasing, had been eager to learn.

And then later, when she had tasted his food, he had felt a warm glow of pride fill his chest. It had felt good to hear her praise, to provide her with pleasure. Unfortunately it had felt a little *too* good. He knew he had to be careful. But that was easier said than done when it came to Ciara Harris.

'How about we give Libby's present a go?'

He watched Ciara pull off the cellophane surrounding Libby's present, and then open the box to reveal a board and cards inside, and considered saying that he had work he needed to attend to.

But the excitement in her eyes when she looked up had him kneeling opposite her.

Reading the instructions, she said, 'Okay, first around the board wins. There are "Truth" and "Dare" cards, all ranked in difficulty from one to five. The player gets to choose the ranking. You can forfeit the "Truth" or "Dare", but that means you do not advance on the board and you also miss your next go. Do you want to go first?'

He studied the cards. What would be the best tactic? Go first and have a head start? Or have Ciara go first so he could learn about the difficulty of the cards from what she selected. He nodded to indicate that he'd go first.

Ciara pointed to the cards set in the centre of the board. 'Truth or Dare?'

'Truth. And I'll go with a level three card.'

Ciara picked up a yellow "Truth" card and read

it out loud. 'Did you have an imaginary friend when you were growing up?'

Oh, hell… This was going to be embarrassing.

He rolled his neck, trying to ignore the way Ciara was studying him expectantly.

He cleared his throat. 'Yes.'

When he didn't add any more, Ciara laughed and said, 'For crying out loud, Tom, you have to tell me more than just *yes*. Was it a girl or a boy? Did he or she have a name?'

He rolled his eyes, cursing the heat of embarrassment that was building on his skin. 'A boy… he was called Arthur.'

Ciara clapped her hands. 'How cute is *that*? How old were you?'

He swallowed hard again and paused, desperately trying to figure out how to answer her question without sounding completely lame.

Ciara's gaze narrowed. 'This is a "Truth" card—you have to spit all the details out.'

'Okay, so he first appeared when I went to boarding school at seven…and he stuck around until I was about twelve.'

Ciara's bright beam morphed into one of disquiet.

Seeing she was about to speak, he interrupted

her, 'And, yes, I *know* twelve is much too old for an imaginary friend. Now it's your turn. Truth or Dare?'

Soft brown eyes held his. 'Was he a good friend?'

He blinked at the gentleness of her tone. The understanding behind her question. She knew how much he had hated school.

Arthur had seen him through the dark nights when he had longed to be at home, hearing Kitty and Fran argue, watching his mother get ready for a night out. Anything but the loneliness, the constant bewilderment he had felt at the jumble of words that had met him every day in the classroom. Arthur had also stood bravely at his side on the rugby pitches, telling him to ignore his father's yells to 'buck up' when he visited on match days.

Now, he answered Ciara's question, 'Yes, he was a good friend—but he did get me into trouble once or twice by persuading me to raid the tuck shop in the middle of the night when he was hungry!'

Ciara shook her head, laughing. 'Everyone needs a friend like that in life. Loyal, but naughty too.'

Their eyes met. Their smiles faded. They had

once been such good friends. Only now did he fully realise how much of a void had developed in his life when he'd lost her friendship.

Pushing those thoughts away, he asked again, 'Truth or Dare?'

'Dare.' She paused and gave him a challenging look. 'And I'm going for a level five.'

'Are you sure?'

She squared her shoulders. Gave him a grin that was much too sexy. 'One hundred per cent.'

'You're determined to win, aren't you?'

'Of course.'

He lifted the 'Dare' card, slowly read the details, wanting to get the words right, and with a satisfied smirk said, 'We'll see about that.' And then he called out, 'You have to perform the snake dance move for ten feet.'

Ciara stared at him. 'No way! You're making that up, aren't you?'

Moving forward, she pulled the card out of his hand. Reading it herself, she studied the pictures beneath the words with a deep frown. They showed a step-by-step guide to performing the dance.

Rocking back on her heels, she shook her head in disbelief. 'God, I thought you were winding me up. The snake dance for ten feet…that's going to be really hard.'

'So, I guess you'll forfeit?'

Her eyes narrowed at his grin. 'Not a chance.'

Standing, she moved to the side of the room next to the drawn curtains. There were no obstacles here, in the walkway that had been created to allow easy movement from one end of the thirty-foot room to the other. He stood when she disappeared behind a sofa and went and stood by the room's grand piano, which would be roughly the finish line for her ten feet challenge.

Ciara was kneeling on the floor. Gathering her hair, she twisted it into a makeshift bun. Then she rolled her shoulders, limbering up.

'Have you ever tried this before?'

Lifting her hands, she positioned them either side of her chest. 'Nope.'

Then, falling forward, she planted both hands on the floor and jerked her body forward. She moved about five inches in total. Five awkward inches that were more sack-of-potatoes-being-shifted than fluid dance move.

She tossed her head. 'Don't you *dare* say a thing!'

He swallowed a laugh.

She gave him a glare before dramatically dropping her forehead to the rug with a groan.

And then he heard her laughter. Her whole body shook.

He sat down on the rug beneath the piano and called to her, laughing too, 'Come on, Ciara, you can do it.'

She lifted her head. Laughed even more. A deep, belly-aching laugh.

A burning urge to go to her, to hold her, to lie next to her, grabbed him by the throat. He winced at its intensity, at how deeply connected he felt to this woman he had so badly let down.

Further down the room, Ciara muttered to herself, 'There must be a knack to this...'

Tom studied her. 'Perhaps brace your toes on the floor behind you and push yourself forward when you lift your chest.'

She looked at him dubiously but followed his advice. This time she shifted forward for close to ten inches. It earned him an elated beam. Her next attempt was less successful. But inch by inch she moved towards him, her cheeks rosy with exertion and laughter.

When she finally reached him, she breathlessly high-fived him.

He pulled her to him for a congratulatory hug. They parted slowly. *Too* slowly.

Ciara held his gaze and through a soft smile said quietly, 'Thanks for the encouragement… You didn't have to help me. We are competitors after all.'

'I couldn't resist helping you—you looked pretty incredible down there.'

The heat in her cheeks flamed at his words.

She went to say something in response, but then stood and fled back to her side of the ottoman. 'It's your turn. Which do you want?'

'Certainly not Dare, after your experience—I don't fancy paragliding off the tower or anything like that. I'll stick with Truth…level five.'

She gave him a wicked grin. 'So I'm not the only one out to win.' Lifting a 'Truth' card, she read, 'What's the silliest thing you have an emotional attachment to?

He threw himself down opposite her. 'Oh, give me a break.' He gave her a deadpan look. 'I don't *do* emotional attachments.'

She wasn't having any of it. She folded her arms. 'First off, Tom Benson, don't blame me… I didn't set the questions. Secondly, it was *you* who asked for a level five, so deal with it. And thirdly, don't even think about not answering truthfully.'

With an exasperated breath he whipped his wallet out of his back pocket. Opening it up, he passed to her the small piece of paper he kept folded in there.

He watched as she unfolded the tattered edges. On the page was a delicate tiny life-size drawing of a pink five-petalled flower.

'I had forgotten about this—my drawing of the Lesser Centaury we found in the woods that day...'

She paused and looked at him. Her gaze shot back to the page. She had drawn the flower on an exceptionally warm July Sunday, when they had sneaked out to swim in the lake and later walk to their favourite spot in the woods. Insects had hummed around them as they'd lain in the warm grass, the air heavy with the scent of woodland and grass and summertime growth. They had kissed. And then slowly made love for the first time.

Her gaze swept back to his. She tried to speak but in the end all she could do was give him a sad smile.

Slowly she folded the paper again. Passing it

back to him, for the briefest moment she leant into him, pressing her lips against his cheek. 'Thank you.'

And then she was pulling away.

'My turn. I want a Truth. Level five.'

For a moment he was disorientated. He wanted to talk about the past. He wanted to have her lips against his skin again. But neither made any sense, so he tucked the paper back into his wallet and picked up the next 'Truth' card on the deck.

He read it twice to himself and then read it out loud. 'What is your deepest fear?'

Ciara's eyes narrowed scornfully. 'What a daft question. I don't know—the world's chocolate supply running out, heights, walking down the street with my skirt tucked into my underpants.'

He laughed, but there was a defensiveness to her expression that had him saying, 'I'm calling cop-out.'

She eyed him unhappily. 'I see nothing wrong with my answer.'

'I hate rats, but they aren't my deepest fear.'

She looked at him curiously. 'So what *is* your deepest fear?'

How would she react if he said *Daring to fall*

*in love with you again*? Would she laugh? Tell him he had no right to do so?

He fixed her with a steady gaze. 'You're not switching this around on me—it's your question. Answer it honestly.'

Her face set into a stubborn expression. 'I don't have any fears.'

Despite her sceptical bravado he could tell that the question had clearly unsettled her. 'Why are you being so defensive?'

Her mouth dropped open, as though she was deeply affronted. 'I'm not—who goes around talking about their deepest fears, in the name of God? I've never done it and I certainly won't start now.'

'With me, you mean?'

She blinked at that, the stubbornness in her eyes giving way to uncertainty. 'It's been twelve years, so…' She trailed off.

'So why would you trust me?'

She grabbed the deck of cards and focused her gaze on them. 'Don't take it personally—it's an Irish thing… We like to pretend everything is grand even when it's clearly not.' She looked back at him, gave a wry smile. 'We don't open our hearts easily, and talking about our emotions brings us out in a rash. For crying out loud, in my family we can't even compliment each other without throwing in an insult… My mother's favourite way of addressing me is, "Ya big eejit, ya."'

'That sounds familiar.'

She looked at him with wide-eyed surprise, but there was a knowing smirk on her lips. 'Your mother the Duchess calls you an eejit?'

He sighed. 'No—and you know that's not what I meant… I mean that *we're* not great on expressing our deepest emotions either.'

Ciara grimaced. 'It gets a little frustrating sometimes, doesn't it? Having to pretend everything is fine.'

There was a vulnerability in her voice that had him wanting to reach out to her, express some of his feelings for her.

In a low voice he admitted, 'You were the first person I ever really spoke to. You were good at listening… When we split up I missed talking with you.'

Ciara bit her lip, said quietly, 'I missed chatting with you too.'

He swallowed at the honesty in her voice. 'If you ever want to talk…'

She shook her head and gave a rueful smile. 'I think you're going to be too busy with the restaurants and the estate to be listening to *me*.'

'I'll always be there for you...call me any time you want to talk.'

She gave him a dubious smile. 'That's good to know.'

A mischievous glint grew in her eye. 'You know, I much prefer chatting face-to-face with people rather than over the phone. If you keep Loughmore we'll be able to do that—wouldn't that be great?' With a happy chortle she added, 'Now, can we please get on with the game? I'm looking forward to beating you.'

Tom shook his head. 'You're impossible.' Then, with a self-satisfied smirk, he gestured to the board. 'I believe you've just forfeited this go, and the next one, so I'm cruising to the finish line. Hit me with a Dare—level five.'

Ciara threw him an evil look, lifted a card and read it, a wicked grin breaking out on her mouth. 'You must compose a poem. You have two minutes to do so before you have to recite it out loud.'

Tom dropped his head and playfully banged it on the ottoman. 'May I have another card?'

Ciara wasn't going to give him an inch. 'Nope—and you have ninety seconds left.'

He stood and walked away. His back to her, he closed his eyes, desperately searching for inspiration.

Much too soon, from behind him, Ciara called out, 'Your time is up!'

He turned to find her standing close, her arms folded.

'It doesn't rhyme,' he said.

Her grin was wicked. 'No excuses. Come on—I'm waiting.'

He cleared his throat, squared his shoulders. 'There once was a bewitching gardener, Who liked to tantalise her employer, She set out one day, To change his ways, And he could only look on in ardour.'

Ciara opened her mouth. Closed it again. And then she was laughing and high-fiving him. 'That was so terrible it was brilliant!'

They stood grinning at one another. And in that moment Tom knew he was tired of fighting his attraction to her.

He stepped closer.

Her eyes grew wide, initially with surprise and then with something much more carnal.

He placed his hand just above the sharp tilt of her hipbone. 'I've decided I'll be a good sport and let you have a turn, even though you forfeited it.'

She looked at him quizzically. 'What's the catch?'

He stepped even nearer, the pull towards her almost buckling his knees. He lowered his mouth to her ear. 'You can have a Truth question, and the question is...would you like me to kiss you?'

Wide-eyed, high heat in her cheeks, she searched for words. 'But that's cheating...you can't set your own questions.'

His heart thundered to hear the breathless sensuality of her voice. 'It's a special level ten question. If you answer it you get to win the game.'

She pulled in a long, deep breath that sounded like a caress. 'Well, in that case...'

His fingertips touched lightly against the heavy silkiness of her hair. 'Remember...you have to tell the truth.'

Her eyes darkened. Her mouth parted ever so slightly. She tilted her head, edged forward, her eyes focused on his mouth. 'You know the answer to that question already...you're just being cruel in making me answer,' she said.

'I want to hear you say it.'

'Yes, I want you to kiss me.'

The delicate narrowness beneath her ribs, above the flare of her hips, was gloriously feminine. He pulled her to him, his mouth finding her ear. He nibbled her lobe. She buckled against him. His lips moved down her throat, his arm holding her tight against him.

Her fingertips trailed over his biceps, then his chest, until finally they clung to his shoulders.

His lips trailed up over the delicate softness of her throat. She trembled. Called out his name into the silence of the room.

His head spun with the need for her.

But he was not going to rush this.

While his mouth continued its slow trail over the silky skin of her throat his hands skimmed the soft shape of her hips, over the high flare of her bottom.

She tilted into him. Sighed again.

His fingers edged down. Grazed over the point where her dress gave way to the soft skin of her thighs.

'You asked if I wanted you to kiss me... I don't

remember you mentioning anything about torturing me.'

He chuckled at her husky outrage, letting his mouth follow a path to her other ear, feeling his pulse pounding at her murmurs and cries, inhaling her floral scent. His body kicked in remembrance of how sweet, how passionate her body had felt beneath his all those years ago.

He grinned against her skin, and continued to trail his lips against her throat while warning her, 'You're not going to rush me.'

She shuddered again…gave a small cry.

He pulled back, revelling in her desire-fuelled unfocused gaze, the blaze of heat on her cheeks. His mouth hovered over hers. Silently tempting her. Every inch of him was screaming.

And then his lips were on hers.

He groaned at their sweet fullness.

He deepened the kiss. Her lips parted.

He swept into her mouth, pulling her tight against him. Her body—firm, softly flaring—pressed into him. Her hips pressed into his thighs, her breasts against his chest.

He clasped his hands even tighter around her waist. Her hips rocked against him.

Breaking away from the kiss, she ran a tor-turous warm and sensual path of kisses down his throat, her hands clumsily undoing the top three buttons of his shirt. Her lips trailed down his chest, scorching him. He groaned deeply, the noise reverberating around the room.

He stepped backwards, about to lose any sense of control, pulling her with him. He came to a stop when the wood panelling of the room pressed into his back. He twisted her around, pressed her against the wall.

His mouth found hers again. They kissed—an all-consuming, head-spinning, perfect kiss.

She shifted her body beneath his weight and for a few moments he lost himself in her gentle rocking against him. Too weak with longing to pull away. But from somewhere deep inside he finally dredged up enough energy to shift away. Not far. Just an inch or two. But enough to start making sense.

He buried his head in her hair and whispered, 'This is about to get out of control.'

'I think it already has.' Her voice trembled with the effort to speak.

He pulled even further back. Knowing he had to kill this.

Placing a hand on the wall behind her, he gave her a steadying look. 'This isn't going to change my mind about selling Loughmore, you know.'

She blinked, and blinked again, the desire in her eyes fading to comical outrage. She smacked him on the arm. 'Tom Benson…what *do* you take me for?' She waved her hand vaguely between them. 'That…that kiss…had strictly *nothing* to do with you keeping Loughmore.'

'So what *was* it about?'

She tossed her head and darted under his arm. At the drawing room door, she stared at him defiantly. 'It was about me winning the game… nothing more.' Then, with a toss of her head, she added, 'And can I point out that it was *you* who asked the question, so don't be blaming me if you can't handle the consequences. Now, I think it's time we had dessert. Libby won't be happy if she finds out we haven't tried her plum pudding.'

With that she left the room with a confident stride, her head held high.

Tom fell back against the wood panelling. Inhaled deeply.

One more day. Then the rest of the staff would be returning to work.

One more day of resisting Ciara.

He was capable of that, wasn't he?

He was capable of not doing something stupid… of not opening up old wounds and creating new ones…wasn't he?

# CHAPTER SEVEN

THE DOOR OF Daly's Pub was blasted open. A procession of eccentrically dressed people carrying musical instruments walked into the centre of the room. A loud cheer went up from the already assembled customers in the ancient pub that operated not only as a bar but also as a grocer's and hardware store.

Perched at a table beside the open fire, Tom leant towards Ciara, 'What's going on? Why are they wearing those oddly-shaped straw hats?'

Ciara laughed. 'You know what? I actually have no idea! They're called the Wren Boys; its traditional for them to go from pub to pub on the twenty-sixth of December, St Stephen's Day, and play music and collect money for charity.'

The Wren Boys picked up their instruments, and at the command of a teenager, who tapped his bodhrán three times with his wooden tipper, began to play a toe-tapping céilí tune.

Their straw hats were cone-shaped, and hid

many of the faces beneath, but he spotted small Sophie from the kiddies' party, who lowered her tin whistle to wave at him shyly, her red hair giving her away.

He had reluctantly agreed to come here this afternoon, eventually giving in to Ciara's protests that he had worked enough for the day and needed some exercise—the mile walk to the village being a perfect excuse to partake in a hot port in Daly's before they made the journey home again.

He took a slug of his port and looked towards Ciara, who was clapping her hands in time with the music, her eyes blazing with delight. Dressed in jeans and a thick cable-knit cream polo neck jumper, her hair tied back into a high ponytail, she looked radiant.

And he longed to kiss her again.

Which would be beyond stupid.

Selling Loughmore was a difficult enough decision. Adding the complication of Ciara into the mix was simply asking for a whole heap of trouble.

Looking about him, taking in all the faces of the other customers who had all earlier come and shaken his hand, offered to buy him a drink, taking in the old charm of the pub's interior, bursting at the seams with memorabilia and framed newspaper clippings of village events, many based around the castle, he wondered once again at Ciara's motivation for persuading him to come here.

Had yesterday, today, all been just part of her campaign to save Loughmore?

*A kiss between old flames.*

Those words came back to taunt him again.

Or was all this nothing more than a trip down memory lane for her?

He gritted his teeth. He was falling for Ciara. Damn it. What type of fool *was* he? To allow himself to fall for her when she would never love him back after all the hurt and pain he'd caused her.

The jaunty music and clapping flowed around him while a claustrophobic hollowness, panic, grew within him.

When the music had come to a stop, and the collection buckets had been passed around for donations, the Wren Boys left the pub to rousing applause.

Standing, he pulled on his overcoat. 'I need to get back to the castle.'

'But we haven't finished our drinks yet.'

He stepped away from the table. 'It'll be dark soon. I'd prefer to leave now.'

'It's only three—it doesn't get dark for at least another hour.'

With a shrug, he turned and walked out of the pub.

Halfway down the main street Ciara caught up with him, dragging on her green parka jacket. They passed the limestone church built by his forefathers, its grounds covered in a thick blanket of snow, and passed the People's Park, with its bandstand, seeing a few brave families making use of the playground despite the low temperatures—one little boy screaming in delight as his father pushed him ever higher on the swing. They passed a few people who wanted to stop to chat with them, but Tom ploughed on, only giving a quick hello.

It was only when they were behind the high castle walls, in the privacy of the pedestrian walkway to the castle, that he turned to Ciara, the burning need to try to understand what was going on between them propelling his angry words.

'Right—enough games, Ciara. All this...everything you have orchestrated to try to persuade me to keep Loughmore...has to stop right now.'

\* \* \*

Ciara left out an angry breath and studied Tom, totally unamused. What on earth was *wrong* with him? They had left half-drunk drinks behind them in the pub.

Anger, tension, and a frustration she didn't quite understand bubbled away inside her. When she spoke she struggled to keep her voice calm.

'I'm not playing games. Yes, I want you to keep Loughmore. For your sake as much as anyone else's. But I've been totally upfront about that, so how exactly am I playing games?'

Tom worked his jaw and then stormed away, down the path.

With a deep sigh she followed him as he entered Loughmore Woods. Most of the trees were bare, allowing weak shafts of sunlight to land softly on the snow-covered earth, where fronds of bracken poked out as if to say hello.

To Tom's back she called, 'Do you want to know why I like working as a horticulturist? Because plants are so uncomplicated in comparison to you men.'

Tom came to a stop at the top of a small incline in the path. He waited there until she joined him. She tried to keep her expression carefree and unfazed, but there was a darkness to Tom's expression that was making her decidedly jittery.

'At least men aren't Machiavellian in everything they do.'

Ciara gave a huff of disbelief. 'How can I be "Machiavellian" when I've been straight up with you about everything?'

Tom yanked a grey woollen hat from his coat pocket and pulled it on. 'Tell me—have our kisses been just about me keeping Loughmore?'

The hat sat perfectly on his head, moulded to his skull, deepening the silver of his eyes. Her heart lurched in attraction.

How was she going to answer his question? Should she pretend that the kisses were part of her efforts to save Loughmore? That they were meaningless, *hadn't* been glorious and beautiful, *hadn't* kept her awake for the last two nights with wicked thoughts of what they might lead to, *hadn't* wrenched open her heart to this man she had once loved with every fibre of her body?

His eyes held hers… How on earth was she supposed to pretend that his kisses weren't tearing her apart when he looked at her with such hypnotic intensity?

She willed herself to look away, but the need

to be connected with him, to be at one with him, was too great. Her heart was beating solidly against her chest, her throat hot with emotion.

'No, the kisses were different—and so was most of everything we've done over the past few days, Tom. We were friends...' She trailed off as a dawning realisation hit her.

Could it be that she had been fooling herself all along? Pretending that her need, her motivation for spending time with him, was all based on saving Loughmore when the truth was she selfishly wanted to spend time with him?

Tom's mouth settled into a hard line. 'We were more than friends, Ciara.'

She felt herself blush at his softly spoken words.

He inhaled deeply, worked his jaw again, and said, 'You said before you regretted it. Is that true?'

The heat in her throat spread to every limb. She bit her lip, looked down the path, burning with the desire to run but knowing there was no way she was capable of walking away from him. For so many years she had survived by hanging on to the untruths she had convinced herself of—that she had moved on from Tom, that she regretted they had ever become lovers.

But now all those untruths were unravelling.

Yes, she regretted what had happened in the weeks and months following their summer together, but she didn't regret their lovemaking. How could she when it had been so perfect, so exquisite, so soul-connecting and intimate with the man she had loved?

She knew they both deserved to hear the truth spoken out loud. Pulling in some air, she said, 'No, I don't regret it…what we had was special.'

Tom blinked hard. His eyes flitted away in a moment's hesitancy before they returned to her with renewed intensity. 'The rest of the staff are back working tomorrow.'

Her stomach flipped in response to the huskiness of his tone. 'I know.'

Tom looked up at the canopy of bare branches hanging over them, his chest rising and falling heavily. He hit her again with those silver eyes. 'I want to be with you tonight.'

The air whooshed out of her lungs. Tears prickled at the sides of her eyes. This was ridiculous. She should laugh and tell him he was being crazy.

It *was* crazy.

But, looking into those silver eyes, she *knew* this man—knew how honourable and good he was, how alive she felt in his arms, knew the bone-deep connection she felt with him. And she said on a whisper, 'I want that too. But only if you swear to believe that it has nothing to do with you keeping Loughmore.'

'What *is* it about?'

She had no idea. She searched for the right words, but none came. And in that moment she realised that she was tired of thinking. Tired of pretending her body and soul didn't need him, even if it was only going to be for a few precious hours.

In a low voice she answered, 'Maybe it's just about living for the moment…taking happiness when you can.'

For a heartbeat they studied each other. And then they were both moving forward.

Days of tension and attraction and denial, years of memories and longing tumbled together. They kissed furiously, their hands gripping each other.

Tom held her tight against him, his arms imprisoning her. Her head swam at his closeness, the passion in his kiss, the hardness of his body.

Fresh snow had started to fall around them, falling on the burning skin of her cheeks. In silence they walked through the woods and skirted the orchards. Tucked into his side, she felt her body hum, while her heart crashed around in her chest in anticipation…and disbelief.

She greedily pushed away all thoughts as to why this was a terrible idea and instead felt liberty for the first time in twelve years. She was going to give her body what it needed. One long sultry night with the man who answered her every physical need.

They entered the castle via the main entrance.

Storm bounded noisily towards them in greeting, pawing the leg of Tom's trousers and clearly unimpressed that his full attention was on Ciara, who was pressed against the giant wooden door, about to collapse beneath the force of his kisses.

With a groan Tom broke away to greet Storm, and when the dog finally pottered away he held her hand and together they rushed up the stairs.

He took her to his bedroom suite. Inside, he kissed her, undressed her. Laid her down in her bra and panties beneath the canopy of his four-poster bed and ate her up with hungry eyes.

'You're even more beautiful than I remember.'

She squirmed at the wonder in his voice, at the need darkening his expression. She held her hand out to him, wanting him at her side, lying on top of her. She wanted to scream with her need for his uplifting, soothing, reassuring weight.

Yanking off his clothes until only his denims remained, he knelt at the base of the bed. Ciara gasped when his lips gently landed on her bluebell tattoo, and then her ankle. Slowly he trailed kisses up her calf, murmuring words about the pleasure he found in her body.

It was torture.

Sensual torture.

She wanted him beside her. She wanted his mouth on hers. His hips rocking against hers. She begged him to stop. But he refused. She writhed as his lips moved onwards, over the delicate skin of her inner thighs. She gasped once again when he went even higher, gasped in disappointment when his lips merely skimmed over her panty line before his lips and tongue began to wreak havoc on her stomach. She arched upwards when his lips landed on the exposed valley of her breasts, his cheek rough with evening shadow brushing intentionally against her stinging nipple.

Unable to take any more, she wrapped her hands around his head and hauled him up to her. She tugged his head down, found his mouth with her lips, groaned deep and heavy at the sensation of tasting him, feeling the elation of his weight spreading across her limbs.

When he entered her, her body arched and her heart broke open with more than a decade full of emotion. Afterwards, lying in his arms, her heart was confused. But he kissed away her vulnerability and made love to her again, with a tenderness that rubbed her soul raw.

Four lousy hours. That was how long Tom had lasted before he had given in to the compulsion to go and seek Ciara out.

He had woken this morning disorientated by the absolute exhaustion in his body but feeling contentment in his soul—only to see the cause of that disorientation about to creep out through his bedroom door.

She had turned when he'd called out to her, her stern pleas for him to be quiet, saying that some staff might already be back at work, at odds with the heat in her cheeks and her darting glances as he moved across the floor to her.

She had begged him to put on some clothes, but hadn't resisted too much when he'd dragged her into his bathroom and undressed her. In the shower they had washed one another. He had gently stroked every inch of her body with a burning need to worship her.

Now, just before lunchtime, despite his pledges to himself that he would play it cool and keep everything that was happening between them casual and relaxed, here he was, searching for her in the gardens with a crazy desperation to see her again.

He eventually found her in one of the glasshouses, bent over a table full of plant trays. She did not respond when he called out her name.

He stood watching her, a jolt of pleasure streaming through him at the memory of looking up into her dazed, passion-filled eyes as she'd straddled him last night, her glorious hair fanned across her naked breasts.

And then, as though sensing him, she turned, tugging out the earbuds from her ears, her smile uncertain.

*Keep it cool and relaxed, Tom. No pressure. Don't expose yourself.*

'Hi, I thought I'd come and see how you're doing...'

*That was the right balance between being a gentleman, caring for a woman you'd slept with, and being casual, wasn't it?*

For a moment she looked nonplussed, unsure of what her response should be, but then, gesturing to the trays on the table behind her, she answered, 'I'm just checking on the winter salads—Libby wants to use them for the starter at the New Year's Eve ball.'

He plucked some rocket from one of the trays. Sweet but peppery, it tasted amazing. 'This is really good.'

Ciara ran her hands over the tall glossy leaves of a tray of Swiss chard. 'We're really proud of the quality of the vegetables and fruit we grow here. In fact, we're now supplying some of the top restaurants in Wicklow and Dublin.'

She paused, turned towards him and fixed her hair behind one ear. He was immediately on the alert. Ciara always touched her hair when she was about to say something she was uncomfortable about.

'I've been thinking—'

He interrupted her with a groan.

She gave him a stern look. 'Let me make it clear...' She reddened and waved her hand vaguely between them. 'What I'm about to say is in no way connected with last night, before you start accusing me of some great Machiavellian plot. It's merely a suggestion.'

She shifted further away to the end of the table, which was lined with trays of Mizuna.

'I understand now why you have to sell Loughmore, but maybe there's a way around it. You've seen the quality of the organic produce we grow here in Loughmore—why don't we grow even more? And, I don't know if you remember, close to the village there's an old barn that could easily be converted into a restaurant—why don't you open a Tom's here? The castle could be opened up during the months you aren't here too. Tours could be given and I can run workshops on wildflowers and heritage plants. And those old stables that aren't used any more would look fantastic converted into shops. Libby's sister Heather is looking for a suitable location to open an art gallery, and there are lots of other artists based in County Wicklow who would love the opportunity to work in a community. Tourism is growing in the county all the time. We can tap into it.'

She paused for a breath, her eyes willing him to be as enthusiastic as she was.

'We can make Loughmore financially viable for you.'

If only it was that easy. 'The estate is in too much debt.'

Ciara gave him a contrite grimace. 'Earlier this morning I looked up Tom's restaurants' financial results from last year. I don't understand why you can't service the estate's debts with the profits you have made.'

Taken aback by how much thought she had put into this, but disliking her interference, he let out an angry breath. 'Those profits are being ploughed back into expanding Tom's.' He gritted his teeth. 'I appreciate your input, but the estate has to fund itself.'

'But *why*?'

'They're two separate entities. I don't want to saddle the restaurant business with debt issues my father created.'

She folded her arms and considered him with a puzzled frown. 'But they both belong to you now. They're both *part* of you. You should protect them. You grew one from nothing, which is amazing, but you should equally cherish your inheritance.'

'And what if I said I never wanted to inherit it in the first place?'

'Why would you say that?'

*Because Loughmore reminds me of you, Ciara...of what I did to you. The shame of how I treated you. It reminds me of the baby we lost. It reminds me of how you refused to answer my calls. It reminds me of how you turned your back on me that night in your mother's house and told me you never wanted to see me again.*

'The restaurant trade excites me. The estate doesn't.'

Ciara came and stood beside him. She was wearing a brown padded jacket, the same shade as her eyes, zipped up so that it almost reached her chin. She looked at him with an honesty that took him straight back to his bedroom last night and the way her eyes had clung to his when they'd made love.

'You'll grow to love Loughmore. I know you will. Please don't rush into this decision. Loughmore deserves better. So do you.'

He shook his head, not understanding. 'What do you mean?

'Your dad has just died. You've taken on a huge amount of responsibility on top of the restaurant empire you're already running. It's a lot for one person to manage.'

Her words were hitting raw nerves he hadn't

even known he possessed. 'I've wide shoulders. I'll cope.'

Ciara didn't look convinced. 'Are you *really* ready to let Loughmore go?'

Frankly, he didn't know what he wanted any more. He had left London less than a week ago, intent on selling Loughmore, restoring the estate's finances and for once and for all putting the ghost of his love for Ciara firmly behind him.

He rolled his shoulders, plucked more rocket, ate it and shrugged. 'I believe so.'

Ciara's hand tentatively touched against the sleeve of his wax jacket. 'I'm not trying to give you a hard time. I want to *support* you.'

He swallowed hard, taken aback at just how acutely moved he was by the truth of her words. He pulled her into his arms and hugged her, muttering 'I know.' He took a few seconds' pleasure in her warmth, touching his lips against her hair, before he reminded himself that he was supposed to be acting laid-back and stepped away.

She wrapped her arms tightly about her waist, rocked back on her heels. She wasn't quite able to hold his gaze. 'Last night… Please know that was just about you and me. Nothing about you keeping Loughmore.'

He could not help the grin that grew on his mouth as images of last night flashed before him—her shyness at first when he had undressed her, her gasps as she had lain beneath him calling his name, her body arched into him... 'Did you enjoy it?'

Her eyebrows shot upwards. She looked at him, speechless for a few seconds, and then her lips quirked, 'It was pleasant.'

He moved in next to her. Stared down into her laughing eyes. 'Just *pleasant*?'

She pursed her lips. 'Yes... I think "pleasant" is the right word to describe it.'

He reached for the waist of her jeans, pulling her hips against his thighs. 'Well, we'll have to make it spectacular tonight.'

She blinked in surprise, blushed, but then let out a theatrical sigh. 'I'm afraid there's no tonight. I'm going home now that the roads have been cleared. And Vince has invited me over to have dinner with himself and Danny.'

He lowered his mouth. She tried to resist him but within seconds was melting against him, sighing with pleasure.

He pulled away long enough to mutter, 'Tell Vince he has another guest coming for dinner.'

# CHAPTER EIGHT

TOOTHBRUSH IN HAND, Ciara crept from her bathroom into her bedroom. Was that a car she had heard, approaching the cottage? At her bedroom window she gingerly parted the curtains in time to see the inner light of Tom's four-by-four flick on as he opened the driver's door.

A thousand tiny bubbles of excitement popped inside her. She gave a squeal—and then grinned at her own inanity.

She hadn't expected him tonight. In spite of the fact that he had appeared at her door for the past three consecutive nights.

She had tried objecting, telling him people would find out, but he had refused to listen. And in truth she hadn't put up much of a fight. Not when he was leaving for London in two days.

Their time was running out.

She grabbed that thought and discarded it somewhere deep inside her. She was dreading the emptiness she was going to face, but hungry to grab hold of what little time they did have left.

Wearing a heavy navy overcoat and a peaked tweed hat, Tom made his way up the cobbled garden path and she danced from foot to foot, her body jittery with attraction, her heart dancing to its own peculiar tune. As he neared the front door she raced downstairs in her bare feet.

She grinned at his gentle rapping and inched the door open. 'Shouldn't you be at the castle, entertaining your mum and sisters?'

He leant much too sexily against the doorframe, those silver eyes beneath his peaked hat trailing over her ivory silk dressing gown. 'Looks to me like you were expecting company tonight.'

Okay, so maybe she *had* dressed for him—just in case he decided to make it four nights in a row. But she wasn't going to admit that to him.

She folded her arms, not budging from the door. 'You haven't answered my question.'

'My family were tired after their journey here today. They went to bed early. Now, are you going to let me in?'

Ciara's heart thudded at the dark desire in his eyes. 'What if they find out you've come here?'

He shrugged. And then gave her the sexiest

grin ever. 'Do you know what I want to do with you tonight?'

She gulped. 'No—what?'

He nodded towards the dying fire, glowing softly in the hearth. 'First I'm going to get that fire blazing again.' Raising his right hand, he went on, 'Then I'm going to open this champagne.' Searching his coat pocket, he extracted a smaller bottle, filled with pink body lotion. 'And then I'm going to lay you down before the fire, undress you ever so slowly, and massage every inch of your gorgeous body.'

Ciara dragged in a shaky breath, trying to calm the pressure of excitement and longing weighing heavily in her bones.

'I must admit I'm in need of a massage. There was a lot of snow that had to be cleared away on the grounds today, in preparation for the ball tomorrow night. I was thinking of booking in for one tomorrow at the local spa.' Swinging the door open, she gave him a cheeky grin. 'But I guess you'll save me the trip.'

Later, they lay on her sofa, covered in a thick throw, Tom's warm body wrapped tightly against hers.

A sigh of pleasure escaped from deep inside her.

Behind her Tom chuckled, his lips gently kissing and teasing her neck.

She snuggled into him, loving this moment of feeling desired, protected, safe.

His lips moved to her ear. She blushed even more fiercely when he began to list all the parts of her body he adored.

She laughed as his list went on and on. Then, turning to him, she shook her head teasingly. 'Tom Benson, you're such a charmer.'

That earned her another wicked grin.

And then his mouth was on hers. His kiss was gentle. Tender. His hand moved slowly over her bare skin…a delicate caress. She pulled away, unable to handle just how vulnerable and confused it made her feel.

She gave a smile, trying to pretend all was fine when in truth she was beginning to feel really scared. His silver eyes held hers and she flipped onto her back, afraid of what he might see.

'So, are you coming to the ball tomorrow night?'

Ciara twisted her head back at his softly spoken question, her heart plummeting. The real world was out there, ready and waiting to point out why all this was a really bad idea.

Grabbing her dressing gown from the floor, she pulled it on. Standing, she backed away from the sofa and, despite the growing panic swirling in her stomach, laughed and rolled her eyes.

'Of course I'm not going. As I've told you plenty of times over the past few days, I'm a member of staff—I don't belong at the New Year's Eve Ball!'

Seeing his expression harden, she felt compelled to fill the tense silence that followed.

'I'm not sure how the other staff would react—or anyone else for that matter. How would we explain it to your family? It's better that I don't go, but I'm sure you'll have a wonderful night.'

Reaching for his trousers, Tom tugged them on. 'We don't need to explain our actions to others. We're grown adults. But if it makes you happy we can say your invitation is my way of thanking you for keeping me company over Christmas.' She was about to speak but Tom got there before her. 'I've also invited Vince and Danny. I thought you'd like to have them there.'

Grabbing hold of her nightdress, that was still on the floor, she wrapped it in a tight ball and placed it on the stairs. 'I really don't want to go. It's not a good idea...' She trailed off, seeing Tom's mouth flatline into a grimace.

The New Year's Eve ball was, by all accounts, a spectacular affair. She should be jumping at the chance of going. And she'd have Vince and Danny for company. But it would deliver her smack-bang into the reality that she didn't belong in his world of wealth and power and social etiquette.

'I don't understand why you're inviting me.'

Tom paused in buttoning his shirt. His hands dropped to his hips.

Standing there, bare-foot, his trousers slung low on his hips, his open shirt exposing the knotted muscles of his abs, the smooth firmness of his chest, Tom eyed her with incredulity. 'Are you *serious*? After the past few days—what we've shared—how could I *not* invite you?'

Oh, God, why had she opened this can of worms? Why hadn't she just made up some excuse as to why she couldn't go, rather than argue the point with him? Now they were heading in the direction of needing to have 'a talk' about how this would all end rather than just saying goodbye to one another...however *that* was supposed to have worked.

She hadn't put much thought into it, unfortunately. Oh, Lord, it was going to be awkward and horrible. She inhaled against the panic growing inside her, the sickening loneliness coating her heart.

'It's very honourable of you to invite me, but I honestly wouldn't have been offended if you hadn't. I had no expectations that you would do so. We both went into the past few days with our eyes wide open—we knew it was just two old flames rekindling what they'd once had. Let's not complicate it.'

A dash of red grew on Tom's cheeks, highlighting the sharp curve of his cheekbones. 'I'm inviting you as a friend. I'm hoping you'll enjoy the ball and have fun. And, as I said already, it's my way of thanking you for your company over Christmas.'

Ciara was about to say something, but Tom got there before her, a sharpness to his voice, 'And before you even think it, never mind *say* it, I don't mean that I'm thanking you for your company in bed.'

Plucking the now empty champagne glasses off the floor, she felt her resolve not to go to the ball wane. It was obviously important to him, and she knew she should accept his invitation graciously, without making a huge song and dance over it.

Straightening, she gave him a warning look. 'Well, if I manage to insult one of the guests or commit some other social faux pas you have only yourself to blame.'

His expression remained grave but his eyes crinkled ever so slightly. 'You won't—and even if you do you're so adorably sincere people will forgive you.' Moving next to her, he placed his hand on her waist and said quietly, 'I'm glad you're coming.'

She gave a wobbly smile. The feeling that events were overtaking her, that she no longer had any control of her life and how she felt for this man, was weighing heavily on her chest.

Tom disappeared into the kitchen, but soon returned with the champagne bottle. 'We have at least half a bottle to finish.'

Part of her wanted nothing more than to spend the night with him, to go upstairs and lose herself physically with this man who managed to turn her inside out. But another, more vehement part of her demanded she start protecting herself. Sleeping with him was stripping away every protective layer she had wrapped around herself in the years following their split.

She forced herself to give him a playful grin.

'I reckon I need my beauty sleep tonight. Time for you to head home.'

Tom looked at her, bemused.

She moved to the front door.

Tom did not follow.

She tried not to wince at the confusion, the hurt in his eyes… It was just his male pride, wasn't it?

He turned and yanked on his sweater and overcoat before joining her at the door. He eyed her unhappily for a brief moment, before turning his attention to unlatching the door.

'I'll be tied up with the arrival of our guests, so I probably won't see you tomorrow, but I'll come and collect you for the ball at seven.'

'You'll be busy. I'll make my own way there.'

He shook his head. 'I'll collect you at seven.'

Then, with the briefest of kisses on her cheek, he walked away. She bolted the door to the sound of his car's engine roaring to life, and as she made her way upstairs she heard the powerful car eat up the silence of the night as it furiously climbed the valley's track.

The Loughmore New Year's Eve ball was every bit as fabulous and glamorous as Ciara had heard.

Pre-dinner drinks had been served in the Great

Hall, to the accompaniment of a string quartet. And the five-course dinner, which had featured crab cappuccino to start, followed by a winter consommé, then a main course of tender slow-cooked ox cheek, and salted caramel tartlets and a selection of Irish cheeses to finish, had taken place in the candlelit Orangery.

Guests had then been invited to the Ballroom for dancing, but she had yet to make her way there—thanks to Vince and Danny's insistence that she join them in the Garden Room, which had been converted into a cocktail bar for the evening. There they had soon joined a raucous table of Tom's friends from London, who were partaking in drinking games much to the enjoyment of Danny.

Vince was on call, so unable to drink, and Ciara had taken part in one game but called it quits after that, finding the bitter alcohol not to her liking.

Now, as she watched Danny and Vince lean in towards the table, sharing jokes and anecdotes with the rest of the group, she sent up silent thanks that they were at the ball. Without them she would have felt at a loss, surrounded by the confidence and social ease of all the other guests, the majority of whom seemed to know one another.

Unfortunately some seemed to remember her too, from their visits to the castle over the years, and she had had to explain that, yes, she *was* still a staff member, which had received various levels of response, but mostly taken aback surprise—whether because she still worked on the estate or was a guest at the ball, she wasn't sure.

Earlier that day she had called Tom to say she had organised for Vince and Danny to collect her from her cottage for the ball, thereby freeing him to spend more time with his guests.

After a long pause he had said, 'If that's what you'd prefer.'

She had grimaced at the coolness of his response but known it was the right call. Last night, after he had left, she had realised just how bad an idea it was for him to collect her. It would send all the wrong signals—make their relationship look like something more than friendship.

She had to think of the future—of living in Loughmore with the speculation of others about her relationship with her employer. It would be horribly awkward. Not only with the rest of the staff but also in her interactions with his family.

And what if he went ahead with his decision to sell Loughmore? How would her colleagues react if they knew they had once been lovers? Would they blame her somehow for his decision to sell?

When Vince and Danny had turned up at her door she had never felt more grateful for their playful *joie de vivre*. Danny had fussed over her hair, insisting it hang loose rather than remain in the bun she had twisted it into, and the two of them had bustled her out through the door, refusing to listen to her doubts as to whether she should attend the ball at all.

On their arrival at the castle she had felt a dizzying confusion of emotions as she had stood in line, waiting to be greeted by Tom and his family in the entrance hall. Giddiness at just how handsome he looked in a midnight-blue tuxedo, his hair sleeked back, had had her skin blushing in memory of their recent lovemaking.

But there had also been that persistent feeling of being an imposter—of not belonging at the ball. And worse still the overwhelming loneliness, the sense of distance and detachment that had come as she'd observed him, so calm and distinguished in his role as Duke. She would always be an outsider in that part of his life.

Tom had headed the welcoming line and had greeted both Vince and Danny warmly. When it had been her turn his eyes had held her gaze for a brief, blazing second before his mouth had murmured against her ear, 'You look stunning.'

Thrown by how she had longed to step towards him, to have him wrap his arms around her, she had darted backwards and caught his mother, who was next in line, gazing at her curiously.

Reddening, Ciara had stepped forward, forgetting that she should wait for Tom to introduce her in her panic and said, 'Your Grace, my name is Ciara Harris. I'm a horticulturist employed here at Loughmore.' At this the Duchess's eyebrows had risen and Ciara had heard herself say, 'Years ago I worked here as a cleaner. My grandparents were Jack and Mary Casey...'

The Duchess had continued to gaze at her curiously. Darting a glance at Tom, who had been staring at her with a perplexed expression, Ciara had felt compelled to explain her presence at the ball.

'Tom invited me tonight as a friend...we used to hang out together during the summer.' Then, at a loss as to what else to say, she'd smiled wanly at the other woman.

The Duchess, her dark brown hair tied back in a chignon, her make-up subtly but beautifully applied to her perfect ivory skin, had given the tiniest hint of a smile, 'Of course I remember you, Ciara.'

Thrown by the gentleness of the Duchess's tone, Ciara had nodded and then scurried away, cringing inside at her runaway mouth and lack of social graces.

She had only seen Tom from a distance for the rest of the night. Which was understandable. He had a hundred and fifty other guests to attend to. And in truth she had been avoiding him.

He was leaving for London tomorrow.

She inhaled a deep breath. She had walked into this situation knowing all along that getting involved with Tom again was asking for trouble. Well, trouble was here, with a capital T, and she had no one but herself to blame for the loneliness blossoming in her chest. She had to deal with it whether she liked it or not.

She stood and held her hand out to Vince. 'Come and dance with me.'

Tom followed his mother as she walked towards the door of the ballroom, concerned at the tiredness etched on her face. He caught up with her by the Christmas tree positioned to one side of the wide double doorway, saw the white flashing lights from the tree emphasising the dark circles under her eyes. He hesitated, thrown by the vulnerability in her expression.

He cleared his throat. 'Would you like to dance?'

His mother blinked. Swallowed. 'Thank you, but I'm feeling rather tired. I know it's probably rude of me, but I'm going to retire for the night.'

Tom placed a hand on her forearm, this new softness and openness in his mother since his father's death still disarming him. 'Tonight…all of Christmas…must have been difficult for you.'

His mother nodded, and then in a low voice said, 'I miss him… As you and I both know, your father had his faults—but I did love him.'

Her hand came to rest on his arm, an action so surprising, given her history of little physical contact with her children, that his heart leapt wildly in his chest.

'Darling, why don't you ask her to dance?' she said.

'Ask who?'

His mother nodded towards the dance floor,

where Ciara was dancing with Parker Kidston, an old schoolfriend of his.

'Ciara Harris, of course.'

Ciara's dress swirled around her calves as Parker twisted her around and around, the gold threads in the white silk catching the light from the overhead chandeliers. Her hair, loose around her bare shoulders, shone in the light too, its rich autumnal tones reminding him of their walk back to the castle through the woods after Daly's Pub, her body tight against his, their steps in perfect harmony.

Now, as he watched her laugh when Parker twisted her beneath his arm, jealousy punched him square in the stomach. 'Why would I do that?'

His mother's cornflower-blue eyes settled on his. 'Because I saw how you looked at her earlier in the Great Hall.'

He looked away from his mother's gaze and back towards the dance floor. Last night when Ciara had asked him to leave there had been a distance in her eyes, in her voice, that had chilled him. The same earlier, when she had called to say Vince and Danny would collect her for the ball and there was no need for him to do so. She had sounded remote…keen to end the call.

'It's complicated.'

'I'm sure it is.'

He twisted back to regard his mother, confused by the regret in her voice. 'Don't you disapprove of her, like you did before?'

'When you were teenagers, you mean? Of course I disapproved then—you were nothing more than children. Now who you date is your choice, but I admit I still worry. Your role is a difficult one. You need someone who will support you in good times and bad. Someone who understands the demands of being a duchess. If you marry—and I sincerely hope you do—your wife will not just be marrying *you*, Tom, she'll be marrying this estate and all the responsibilities that come with it. It's a lot to ask of any woman— make sure she's prepared for it.'

Thrown, Tom shrugged and gave a rueful laugh. 'You're jumping the gun…it's early days with Ciara and I.'

For the longest time Tom could ever remember his mother held his gaze. Something shifted in him at the openness, the concern, the love he saw there.

'I don't want you hurt again like you were all those years ago after your last summer here in Loughmore. Am I right in guessing it was because of Ciara?'

Tom nodded in response, and his mother considered him with a remorseful expression. 'I wanted to speak to you. But your father was so cross at the time over your decision to become a chef he asked me not to see you. It's something I deeply regret.'

Sharp pain kicked hard in his chest when he remembered the eighteen-month period after he'd split with Ciara, when he had had no contact with his parents. Unable to hide the bitterness inside him he said sharply, 'I needed your support but you both shut me out.'

His mother winced, but still held his gaze. 'I know. I'm sorry.'

Tom insisted on walking with his mother to her suite. They did so in silence.

Outside her door, she turned to him and said, 'All I wish for you in life is a wife who loves you with all her heart. I didn't have that with your father...it was hard to live with.' Then, with a faint smile, she added, 'But don't rush into any decisions—make sure that the person is right for you. Sometimes we think we can change the person we love, make them something they're not. I thought I could get your father to love me, and in his own way he did, but I never truly had his heart.'

Tom walked away from his mother's suite, heard her door softly closing behind him. He winced in memory of the sadness etched in her eyes.

Back in the ballroom, he grabbed a whiskey from a passing waiter and was soon joined by a group of Fran's old university friends, whom he knew through their frequent visits to Bainsworth over the years. He nodded distractedly at their chatter, his gaze wandering over the dance floor, searching for Ciara. Where *was* she?

He took a gulp of the whiskey, barely noting its burning flow down his throat. He gripped the tumbler tighter, confusion raging through him.

He wanted to be with Ciara, to hold her in his arms again, inhale her vanilla and rose scent. Feel his heart explode with happiness when she smiled. He wanted their sizzling attraction…their friendship. He wanted their chatter and ease.

Why was he doing this? Allowing himself to fall in love with her? He had seen the toll it had taken on his mother—to be in love with a man who didn't love her back with the same intensity and need and intimacy.

It was happening already—Ciara was pushing him away, distancing herself from him. Tonight whenever he'd caught her eye she'd looked away. What had happened twelve years ago was about to happen all over again.

His stomach lurched at that thought.

But he had no one to blame but himself.

From the stage, the lead singer of the band announced that there were only fifteen minutes until midnight. She invited the guests to collect their coats from the cloakroom in order to welcome the New Year out on the terrace.

Tom shook himself. He was the host of this party.

He beckoned the guests towards the cloakroom, and out in the Great Hall accepted Stephen's offer of his overcoat and allowed Kitty to drag him out onto the terrace.

Laughing, Ciara ran with Vince down the corridor to the temporary cloakroom, stopping when she almost lost one of her shoes.

'Hurry up—we're going to miss the midnight celebrations.' Vince urged her on.

He had found her in the kitchen, sharing a pot of tea with Libby. She had popped in to say hello and had found herself staying there for well over half an hour, glad to take refuge in the familiar surroundings of Libby's kitchen after seeing Tom and his mother deep in conversation in the ballroom, their glances constantly shifting in her direction.

What had they been saying? Had his mother learnt about their relationship? Was she warning him about the inappropriateness of getting involved with a member of staff?

At the cloakroom, Vince eyed the attendants, Kelly and Sinead, who were closing the cloakroom door. 'Sneaking out to watch the fireworks, girls?'

When both the girls reddened and mumbled 'yes,' Vince laughed. 'Good for you.' Nodding towards the near empty coat racks beyond the partially open door he added, 'I see we're the last to head out. Can Ciara and I have our coats as quickly as you can?'

Then, running back to the ballroom, they joined the rest of the guests out on the terrace.

The crowd were already assembled into one large circle that extended around the entire periphery of the forty-foot-plus flagstone terrace.

The band had also moved out onto the terrace with their instruments, and the lead singer called out on the portable microphone. 'It's twenty seconds to midnight, folks!' and then began the countdown.

Vince led Ciara through the crowd until he found Danny. They joined the circle of partygoers, Ciara holding Vince's hand on one side before sharing a smile and holding hands with the elderly gentleman on her other side.

'Five, four, three…' the crowd called out.

Ciara's gaze darted around the crowd. Where *was* he?

'Happy New Year, everyone!' the lead singer called out.

Desperation took hold of Ciara. She wanted at least to be able to *see* him.

And then she spotted him, further down the circle, embracing Kitty, shaking the hands of others around him. He was smiling. Relaxed. Everything she wasn't.

The band began the opening bars of 'Auld Lang Syne.' Ciara's heart fell heavily.

The crowd around her began to sing. She joined in for the first few lines. '"Should old acquaintance be forgot, and never brought to mind...?"' But the words, not for the first time, choked her.

She shut her eyes for a moment and then glanced towards Tom. Everyone around him was singing but, grim-faced, he was staring in her direction.

She winced.

For a crazy moment she wanted to go over and stand before him and yell, *Do you know that every year I thought of you when I sang those words? That I had to leave every party early, afraid that if I started crying I would never stop? Do you know I missed you that much, Tom? Did you even think of me? Why did we ruin what we had by sleeping together? Why was I stupid enough to fall in love with a man I could never be with...who when faced with the prospect of being tied to me for ever through our baby looked dismayed.*

She broke her gaze away. Sighed with relief when the singing stopped and the fireworks spectacular began. The crowd gasped as the sky lit up in a symphony of red and blue explosions, the colours catching the sparkling snow still blanketing Loughmore…

Fireworks over, Tom was talking to an old friend of his father's in the Great Hall while handing his coat to an awaiting Stephen when Ciara approached him in a rush.

Giving Lord McCartney an apologetic smile, she said, 'My apologies for interrupting, but I just wanted to say thank you for a wonderful evening. I have to leave now—'

Tom took her arm. 'David, will you excuse me for a moment? Ciara and I need to talk.'

He led her in the direction of the Morning Room, biting back the temptation to demand to know why she was leaving early until they were behind closed doors.

But when he threw open the doorway of the room he came to a stop. Fran was perched on one of the sofas, the voluminous skirt of her red taffeta gown spread around her, surrounded by a bevy of friends. Empty champagne bottles were strewn across every surface.

Fran gave a squeal of excitement, followed by

a little hiccup. 'Tom! Come and join us! We were just discussing the Somerset Ball.' Smiling at a group of friends seated on the opposite sofa, she added, 'The girls were all wondering if you plan on attending. Isn't that right, Alicia?'

Alicia Percy-Villiers gave Fran a vile look, which only caused Fran to laugh in delight. Then Alicia stood and regarded him, while smoothing out the gold silk of her ball gown. 'We missed you in St Moritz this year.'

Alicia's gaze wandered towards Ciara. As did Fran's. Fran stood and walked towards them. 'I'm Fran—Tom's sister. I don't think we've met before…' Pausing, Fran considered Ciara. 'Although I must say you *do* look familiar.'

Beside him he felt Ciara stiffen. Sharply he said, 'Ciara is a friend of mine.'

Ciara, reddening, cleared her throat. 'I worked here during the summer as a teenager—that's why you recognise me.'

Fran slapped her own cheek lightly and rolled her eyes dramatically. 'Of *course*—Ciara. I should have remembered you. Gosh, I reckon I might need to lay off the champagne for a while. What are you doing now?'

There was an awkward pause before Ciara answered. Everyone in the room was waiting for her response. 'I'm still working here—now in the gardens.'

Fran's gaze ran from Ciara to Tom and then back to him again. She was clearly trying to understand exactly what was going on between him and the gardener. 'Cool.'

The faces of the rest of the guests in the room held the same expressions of curiosity.

Hating their interest, hating the pointless class divide that had Ciara constantly feeling the need to explain her presence in his company, he said sharply, 'Ciara is a respected and much sought after horticulturist—we're lucky to have her here in Loughmore. Her research into rare and heritage plants has been published in many scientific journals.'

Ciara looked at him, aghast, while the rest of the people in the room stared at them with a hint of scandalised interest.

Ciara moved towards the door. 'I need to go. Vince is waiting for me.'

Placing a hand on Ciara's arm, to prevent her leaving, he turned to his sister. 'Fran, Ciara and I need to speak in private.'

Fran made a playful noise of intrigue, determined to tease him. 'Oh, now that sounds *very* mysterious.'

Fran's laughter died, though, when he hit her with a glare.

Beckoning her friends to the door, she said, 'I reckon it's time for us to hit the dance floor.'

The group slowly made their way out of the room.

When she passed them by Alicia gave him a coy smile and said, 'You still owe me a dance from the Rhodes ball, Tom.'

When he shut the door on their laughter and calls for more champagne Ciara folded her arms and regarded him crossly. 'For her sake, I hope Alicia is wearing steel-toecap shoes.'

He ignored her jibe and asked instead, 'Why are you leaving?'

Her mouth tightened. She looked as though she was in the mood for a fight. *Good.* Because so was he.

'I don't need you defending me by exaggerating the importance of my job,' she said.

'Some people need to be educated and taken off their high horses. And I wasn't exaggerating. Don't forget I have access to your personnel file—your CV is very impressive. Now, are you going to answer my question?'

She yanked the belt of her long camel-coloured wool coat tighter. 'Vince wants to call in to see Paddy Hayes—he's eighty-five and lives on his own. He hasn't been well recently and Vince wants to check up on him, give him some company. It's sad to think of him all alone on New Year's Eve. I said I'd take a lift home with himself and Danny on the way.'

She stared at him defiantly, the pink in her cheeks the same shade as the gloss on her lips.

He worked his jaw.

She folded her arms.

The stand-off between them ensued.

But then something dangerous shifted in the air between them. The irritation in her eyes was replaced with a hunger that sideswiped him.

With a curse, he was crossing the short distance between them, his mouth finding hers, his hands frantically undoing her belt. Her coat dropped to the ground. His mouth trailed over the smooth skin of her bare shoulders, his hands on the silk of her gown, pulling her tight against him.

He heard himself whisper, 'I've been wanting to do this all evening.'

Against his ear she moaned deep in her throat, her body shuddering against his. Breathlessly she whispered, 'I need to go. Vince is waiting for me.'

His mouth captured hers again. She kissed him back wildly, her hands running through his hair.

They kissed, hard and furious, hot desire moulding their bodies together.

He pulled away long enough to mutter, 'I'll drop you home later.'

His mouth captured the soft pillows of her lips again, but after a few seconds she pushed against him and moved away, shaking her head. 'You're busy. I should go.'

He watched her bend to pick up her coat and that feeling of her closing him out of her life returned with a vengeance. He swallowed the pride that was telling him to let her go and bit out, 'I want to drop you home.'

Her phone began to ring. She grimaced when she pulled it out of her coat pocket. 'It's Vince. I have to go.'

He ground his teeth. 'Why?'

She paused, bit her lip before answering. 'I'm leaving early tomorrow morning for Dublin. I'm spending the day with my mother.'

He folded his arms, trying not to let his surprise at her plans show. He had thought they would spend tonight together—tomorrow too. 'You know I'm leaving for London in the afternoon?'

She winced ever so slightly at his words, but then a hardness came over her expression. Squaring her shoulders, she answered calmly, 'Yes, I know.'

Anger flared inside him. 'Why have you been avoiding me all night?'

'I haven't…' Pausing, she exhaled loudly and tilted her chin defiantly. 'You said you wanted us to part as friends—let's do that.'

'I'm not sure friends sleep together.'

She placed a hand on the console table beside her, leaning her weight against it. Her head dropped, and when she looked up there was no fight left in her eyes.

'Please, Tom. I don't want it to be like twelve years ago. I don't want us to part arguing like this.'

The air in his lungs whooshed out. She was right.

Her phone rang again.

Reaching forward, he took it from her and answered. Told Vince he would take Ciara home himself.

Ciara threw him an angry glance, and when he'd hung up he spoke before she could. 'You're right. I don't want us arguing.' Something rather large seemed to be stuck in his throat at this point, and he had to swallow hard to shift it. 'Come and dance with me.'

She eyed him dubiously. 'But you hate dancing.'

He managed to force a smile to his mouth. 'Yes, but I know how much you enjoy it.'

In the ballroom, he breathed out a sigh of relief that the band were playing an up-tempo song. He guided Ciara out on to the dance floor, where they joined a group of old family friends from Dublin.

God, he hated dancing. But he forced himself to smile, to pretend that he was having a great time. And when the tempo changed to a slow dance he held her in his arms at a respectful distance.

His mind felt numb, but he managed to chat to her about her plans for tomorrow. Told her of the opening of a Tom's in Bordeaux next week. And when she said she'd like to go home he drove her there, through the white silence of the snow-covered countryside.

He walked her to the door with a sense of unreality.

She opened her front door and turned to him. In the darkness she gave him a fleeting smile. 'Thanks for the lift.'

He nodded. Working all the time to keep the conversation light, casual, with none of the pain and hurt of twelve years ago. 'I haven't made my decision on selling Loughmore yet, but you will be the first to know when I do.'

She stepped out of the shadows of the doorway, her expression sad and resigned. 'If there's anything I can do to help, let me know.'

He stepped back, wanting to hold her again, kiss her, but knowing that to do so would be to cross that friendship barrier she so obviously wanted restored. 'I'd better get back to the party. Sleep well.'

She stepped closer again, following him, her eyes holding his with a tender sadness. 'It was a wonderful Christmas.'

He needed to get away. He nodded quickly. 'Yes it was.' And turned away.

'Tom, I...'

Halfway down the path he turned at her call, hope spinning in his chest. 'Yes?'

'I…' She hesitated for a moment and then said quietly, 'Take care of yourself.'

In the car, he sat and watched her close her door and then saw the downstairs lights come on. Already missing her. But knowing he had no option but to move on with his life.

# CHAPTER NINE

'GOD ALMIGHTY, CIARA, you're looking awful—
are you sick?' Standing on the doorstep of her
redbrick terrace house, in pink slippers and a
dressing gown, Ciara's mum eyed her with un-
disguised horror.

Just great. Not only did she feel lousy, but apparently she looked even worse.

Keen to divert her mum's attention, she held
out the bag of gifts she was carrying. 'Happy
New Year, Mum.'

Her mum whisked the bag out of Ciara's hand.
'Ah, love, you shouldn't have. You know I didn't
want anything.'

With her mum busy rifling through the bag
Ciara took the opportunity to slip into the house,
muttering, 'I could kill for a cup of tea.'

While Ciara boiled the kettle her mum fussed
around her.

'Will you have a mince pie, pet? Or how about
some of your gran's Christmas cake? She posted

it to me all the way from Renvyle. I told her not to, but as usual she didn't pay a blind bit of notice to what I said. For the cost of posting it I could have bought ten of them in Dunne's Stores, but would she listen? And I ended up having to go down to the sorting office to collect it because I wasn't at home when my post lady arrived.'

Normally Ciara would have just shrugged at her mum, changed the subject for an easier life, but there was something inside her this morning—was it tiredness from her sleepless night, or a need for some love and understanding in her world, a need for forgiveness and harmony?—that had her turning to her mum and saying quietly, 'Maybe sending the cake is Gran's way of showing you she loves you.'

Her mum leant against the counter-top. 'You really *are* sick, aren't you?'

Ciara rolled her eyes. Mentions of love, affection, or any emotions for that matter were without doubt borderline taboo in her family.

'I only had breakfast an hour ago. That's why I'm not hungry.'

Taking two mugs with bright red poppy designs from a mug tree on the counter, her mum asked, 'Why are you here so early, anyway?'

For a moment Ciara thought about making up an excuse, but instead she spoke the truth. 'I wanted to see you.'

In the process of pouring boiling water into the cups, her mum lowered the chrome kettle to the laminate surface of the counter-top and said, 'Now you've *really* got me worried.'

God, trying to talk to her mother about anything substantial was impossible. Taking some milk from the fridge, Ciara wondered what exactly she was hoping to achieve today.

She had slept terribly. And woken early to an emptiness inside her that was even worse than the night before. So much for her hope of sleeping it off.

She had gone to bed last night determined to start the New Year with strength and resolve—with a determination to put everything about Tom behind her. But she hadn't reckoned on the loneliness that had had her showering and dressing and shooting out through the door in record time.

She had needed to get away from her cottage, from the estate. Away from the hope that Tom might call in to see her one final time. It was all over. Tom was going back to his life in England and the sooner she accepted that fact the better.

Passing the milk to her mum, she said, 'I thought we could go for a walk in Phoenix Park this morning—maybe head to the sales this afternoon.'

'Ah, love, I have the New Year's Day bingo in the parish hall this afternoon.'

'Mum, for crying out loud.'

'What?'

'Can't you for once…? Can't you spend some time with me?'

Was she really saying these things to her mother? Asking her for her company, her support? What was the point? What did she expect? That after all these years she and her mum might actually have a proper conversation that wasn't full of wisecracks and avoidance.

Her mum studied her, her mouth pursed tightly. 'I read in the newspapers that the new Duke was in Loughmore for the Christmas. He's upset you again, hasn't he?'

For a nanosecond Ciara considered answering her mother, but then she moved towards the hallway, muttering, 'I need to go to the bathroom.'

Bounding up the stairs, instead of going to the bathroom she headed into her old bedroom. There she stared at the 'Plants of Ireland' posters she had bought in the National Botanical Gardens for her seventeenth birthday and had later hung on her headache-inducing purple bedroom walls.

Her birthday was in June, and she remembered her seventeenth birthday so well—in particular her ever-growing excitement at the prospect of seeing Tom again. After visiting the gardens—which she had had to drag her friends around—they had gone into Temple Bar where she had got her bluebell tattoo.

Her mum had hit the roof, and Tom hadn't been keen at first, telling her she shouldn't have marked her skin, but eventually he had grown to like it. At least she hadn't got a tattoo of his name, which was what she had *really* wanted to do. Thank God even her seventeen-year-old infatuated self had seen how cringeworthy *that* was. But whenever she looked at her bluebell she thought of the swathes of bluebells that carpeted Loughmore Woods in the springtime—and then, of course, her thoughts turned to Tom.

Out in the corridor she heard her mum going into her bedroom. Part of her didn't want to talk to her mum about Tom. She didn't want to lift the lid on her mum's anger with his dad and with Tom himself. She didn't want to have to put into words the turmoil inside her right now, because to do so would make it all too real, would stop her moving on.

But another part of her *did* want to talk to her mum—the one other person who understood what it was like to fall for someone out of your reach; the one other person who understood what had happened between herself and Tom all those years ago. Part of her wanted to make sense of everything in talking.

But did she seriously think talking to her mum was an option? They just didn't have that type of relationship. Theirs was a 'batten down the hatches' type of relationship, where anything difficult in life was ignored or laughed off with gallows-type humour. And that was not going to change now.

Out in the corridor, she knocked on her mum's bedroom door and went inside when her mum called for her to do so.

Her mum, now dressed in a knee-length plum wool dress, was at the dressing table, brushing her shoulder-length brown hair. Slim, with almond-shaped eyes and cheekbones to die for, she was truly beautiful. Sadness seized Ciara's throat. Her mum had never met anyone after her dad had left them. Did she ever turn the key after a day's work and wish she had a hug waiting on the other side of the door?

She smiled at her mum's reflection. 'Let's head into town. I'll buy you lunch. You can be back in time for your bingo.'

Her mum shifted along the stool she was sitting on, 'Come and put some make-up on.'

Ciara went and sat beside her. 'Do I look that bad?'

Her mum laughed. 'Nothing some war paint can't mend.'

Ciara rolled her eyes, taking the moisturiser and foundation bottles her mum held out to her. 'There's no fear of anyone getting a big head in this house, is there?'

For a few minutes both women worked in quietness, applying foundation and concealer and then working on their eyes.

Her mum pumped at her mascara. But instead of applying it she looked at Ciara's reflection for the longest while.

Thrown by her mum's scrutiny, Ciara lowered her eye shadow brush. 'I don't wear a lot of make-up at work. I'm out of practice.'

Her mum shook her head. Gave her a hesitant

look. 'The night the Duke came here…when we found him on the doorstep… I didn't want to admit it at the time… I was worried about you… but he was genuinely upset. He was very respectful to me, and he apologised for upsetting you. He seemed like a nice person.'

Thrown, Ciara focused on dabbing her brush against the eye shadow palette. 'He *is* a nice person—but that's all in the past.'

Her mum made a disbelieving sound before adding, 'It sure doesn't sound like it is…or look that way, given how pale you are today.'

Emotion fisted in Ciara's chest and she reddened at the gentleness of her mum's voice. For a brief moment they held each other's gazes, feeling a connection forming between them that was as disconcerting as it was wonderful.

Her mum gave a small grimace. 'When he was leaving he said, "I'm sorry for the pain I've caused her…she's everything to me. Please tell her how much I love her." I should have told you.'

Ciara's mouth dropped open. 'He said *that* to you?'

'I didn't tell you because I didn't want you involved with him.'

Ciara edged back on the stool, disbelief confounding her. He had said he *loved* her! To her *mother*! Why had he never told *her*?

But then sense kicked in. He had said those words in the heat of the moment, in the sadness of that night. Even if he had told her himself it wouldn't have changed anything. They were still from different worlds, with their own lives to forge.

Her mum was staring at her, nervously waiting for a response. 'It's okay, Mum, it wouldn't have mattered if you *had* told me. It was all over between us anyway.'

Her mum pumped her mascara again and lifted the heavily loaded wand. She was about to apply it to her eyelashes, but then lowered it again and asked quietly, 'Did you love him?'

Ciara waited a moment for a wisecrack of some sort, but none came. Instead her mum looked at her with empathy, with an understanding that grabbed her heart and tugged hard. She swallowed. 'Yes…yes, I loved him.'

Her mum breathed in deeply. 'What happened over Christmas?'

Her heart was thudding in her chest, and part of her wanted to run away, but somehow she managed to answer. 'We spent it together, but we've agreed to be friends only.' Seeing her mum's deep frown, she added, 'It's not a big deal…it's better this way.'

'Do you love him now?'

'There's no point, is there?'

Her mum didn't look convinced. 'If he wasn't a duke would things be different?'

Ciara grabbed hold of one of her mum's lipsticks. Opening it blindly, she stared at it but failed to register what colour it was before she closed it again.

She gave her mum a rueful smile. 'No. Now, we'd better get a move on or you'll miss bingo later.'

She bolted out of the bedroom and headed downstairs, with the rest of the answer she would have given her mum if they'd been closer—if the words hadn't been too private and painful—spinning around her brain.

*No, things wouldn't be different, because I still wouldn't understand what he feels for me, never mind actually believe that he could ever truly love me… I'm not what he needs.*

A week later Tom threw his overnight bag next to the coatstand in the hallway of his Kensington apartment and sat down onto the parquet floor to cuddle Storm. Storm nuzzled into him, his tail wagging frantically as though Tom had returned from an epic Arctic adventure instead of an overnight stay in Bordeaux.

Tom would have happily sat on the floor all night, taking comfort from Storm's affection, but after a few minutes of indulgence Storm grew bored and padded off—no doubt in the hope of finding one of Tom's ties, which he was partial to chewing.

Standing, Tom read the note left by his cleaner and dog-sitter Helena, assuring him that Storm had been fine in his absence, then rifled through his post. He opened his fridge, decided he couldn't be bothered eating, turned on his laptop and poured himself a drink.

Ten minutes later he switched off the laptop, resigned to the fact he was in no mood to work. He stared instead at the whiskey in his tumbler. It was the twenty-year-old malt Ciara had given him for Christmas.

Today, in Bordeaux, at the opening of Tom's Restaurant in the Bassins à Flot district of the city, he could have sworn he had heard her laughter. He had turned away from the British Ambassador, who had travelled to Bordeaux for the opening, and searched the restaurant, but of course it had all been in his imagination.

The same as it had been when he'd thought he had seen her walking down the Royal Mile in Edinburgh earlier in the week, when the delight in his heart had knocked him sideways, and the bitter disappointment when he'd chased after her to find it was a different person had almost knocked him out.

He missed her.

There were no other words.

He eyed his phone.

She had said they would be friends.

What was the harm in ringing her? As he would with any other friend.

He dialled her number.

A storm of butterflies hit his stomach.

It rang and rang and rang.

He was about to hang up when she answered.

'Tom.' Her voice held surprise, delight, doubt.

He cleared his throat. 'Hi. I thought I'd call... see how you're doing.'

He heard her footsteps on the other end of the phone. Where was she? What was she doing? It felt so wrong to know so little about her day-to-day life. Not to be there with her.

And then it hit him. Square in the eyes. He was in love with her.

He wanted Ciara Harris in his life.

'I'm fine. I was just watching TV with Boru… having a cup of tea.' She paused and gave a little laugh. 'My life must sound so dull to you.'

He was in love with her!

His hands shook, and the sound of her light, musical voice had him saying gently, 'It sounds perfect.'

'It does?'

*Yes, it does. I wish I was sitting there with you. The fire burning. You cuddled against me. Knowing we would soon be going to bed together. Knowing I would have you lying by my side every night for ever and ever. That's what I want most. To know that every night we would lie together, as husband and wife, in our bed, in that cocoon of privacy and love and tender moments.*

Tom shook himself. At a loss as to where all these thoughts and emotions were coming from. At a loss as to just how intense, how powerful, how *real* they were.

'Tell me about your day?' he asked.

They chatted for a while. Ciara told him about the garden tour she had given that morning, to the children from Loughmore School. He told her about his trip to Bordeaux, and the beauty of the city. When he had finished, he wavered, knowing he should get his head straight before he said anything else.

But it was so good to speak with her, to hear her laughter, so he said into the silence of the line, 'I wished you were there with me.'

He heard the tiniest exhalation and then, 'I'd better go…it's getting late.'

He winced, her words as effective as a hand physically pushing him away. Old fears surfaced, and he could not help the bitter note in his tone when he said, 'You haven't asked me about Loughmore—if I've come to a decision over selling it.'

On the other end of the line he heard her pull in a breath. 'I know how difficult it must be for you at the moment, deciding what to do, and I don't want to add to it. You know how I feel about it all, but I'm sure you'll make the right decision—for both you and Loughmore.'

Thrown by her answer, by her acceptance, her

support, her belief in him, he said, 'I'll call you again soon.'

A familiar television programme's theme tune played in the background. Quietly, she said, 'I'm not sure that's a good idea.'

Bewildered he asked, 'Don't you want me to call?'

The theme tune continued to play, and then in a tired voice she said, 'It's too hard saying good-bye.'

Tom stared at his phone, heard the disconnected buzz playing out from the speaker.

She had hung up on him.

His bewilderment switched to anger, then fear, then back to confusion.

What did she mean?

But one thing was for sure: Ciara sounded as lonely as he did.

Why, then, did she keep pushing him away?

Was she as scared as he was of being hurt again?

# CHAPTER TEN

CIARA SHUT DOWN her laptop and tidied away her paperwork, hearing the applause from the gardening and forestry teams at Bainsworth Hall continuing as she did so.

Taking a seat beside Henry Page, Head of Parks and Gardens at Bainsworth, she acknowledged his thanks for her presentation and nodded in agreement when Henry said he was looking forward to increased co-operation between Loughmore and Bainsworth in their joint conservation efforts.

She hoped and prayed she was appearing professional and unruffled to all those assembled in the room, because inside she felt as if she was going to crumble at any moment.

She had been given only two days' notice of this meeting. On Monday morning Sean had casually strolled into the walled garden and told her that Henry Page had called and asked if Ciara would speak at the annual Bainsworth Hall Parks and Gardens team meeting on the topic of heritage planting.

Normally Ciara would have been excited at the prospect of sharing her knowledge and having the opportunity to see the famed gardens of Bainsworth for the first time. But for the past two days a growing knot of despair had taken hold— a knot that had only tightened when the estate car that had met her at the airport had driven through the entrance gates of Bainsworth and along its tree-lined avenue to reveal the astonishing beauty and grandeur of the Palladian-style hall.

To be here, at Tom's primary residence, felt unnatural. Alien, even. It intensified how much she missed him. It emphasised just what a gap existed in the lives they both led.

She still did not know what decision he had taken over Loughmore. Could she take Henry's words as a good omen for what the future held?

She stood as the team began to file out of the converted barn where the day's team meeting had taken place.

'It's a shame you can't join us for dinner, Ciara.'

Ciara gave Henry a smile of apology, checking the time display on her phone. 'My flight back to Dublin leaves in three hours. I'd better leave for the airport soon.'

'A car is booked for you in an hour's time, but first the Duke has requested to meet with you.'

Ciara, in the process of putting her paperwork into her shoulder bag, paused and looked at Henry with consternation. 'He's here at Bainsworth?'

'Yes, he arrived this lunchtime.'

She hadn't known he would be here. She had assumed he'd be in London. She picked up her phone, checked the screen again. 'I don't think I've time—will you give the Duke my apologies?'

Henry walked around the large conference table towards the exit door. 'Don't worry, we'll make sure you get to your plane on time.'

The knot in Ciara's stomach tightened. On wobbly legs she followed Henry out onto the pebbled pathway that ran past the six-acre walled garden of Bainsworth Hall, which she had toured with Henry earlier in the day, and out onto the Italian terraces that ran behind the hall.

A thousand thoughts raced through her mind. Why hadn't Tom told her he would be here? She grimaced as she remembered how she had ended their call last week. What on earth had she been thinking? Why had she admitted just how hard she found it talking to him? Why did he want to meet with her now? Was it to tell her about his decision on the future of Loughmore?

Walking up the central path through the terraces, they passed the vast fountain that sat before the rear entrance portico, its twenty-five water jets filling the air with a faint mist.

After taking the limestone steps up to the portico they entered the hall and passed through a state room full of statuary and tapestries. Ciara tried to listen to Henry's guided tour as they moved through a gilded drawing room with a dazzling royal blue and gold carpet, but she was too nervous to take much in.

Beyond the drawing room, they walked along a wood-panelled corridor filled with marble busts. Henry came to a stop outside an open door and tapped lightly on the wood.

Ciara's heart went into orbit when she heard Tom call out, 'Come in.'

Sitting behind a desk that was positioned before the enormous sash windows of the office, Tom stood when they entered.

Dressed in a charcoal suit and a pale pink shirt,

the top button undone, he looked sexy and powerful, and her mouth grew dry while her heart pounded in her ears. For a brief moment she felt hot tears at the back of her eyes, but she pulled herself together in time to say, 'Your Grace...' following Henry's introduction.

Tom rolled his eyes.

Henry looked from Tom to her, clearly confused at Tom's reaction, and then disappeared out of the room.

Tom walked towards her, his gaze travelling down over her navy pin-striped trouser suit, pausing at her red stiletto shoes. Then his eyes captured hers. Attraction zipped between them.

'It's good to see you.'

Goosebumps pebbled on her skin at the huskiness of his tone. How tempted she was to walk towards him, to place her head on his shoulder, wrap her arms around his waist.

Despite the dryness in her mouth, she forced herself to say, 'You too—but I'm afraid my flight to Dublin leaves soon, so I'd better get going.'

'It sounds as though you can't wait to get away from me.'

Despite his teasing tone, there was a strain in Tom's expression that grabbed her heart. 'What?

No! I'm just worried about my flight, that's all. I didn't know you would be here, that you would want to meet with me. You should have told me.'

He shrugged and went and shut the office door. 'Would you have come if you'd known I'd be here?'

Thrown by his closing the door, and by his tone—which implied he already knew the answer to his question—Ciara studied him, realisation slowly dawning. 'Was it your idea for me to come here? To speak to the gardening team?'

He came closer...too close, in fact. She could smell his aftershave, and every cell in her body melted as the image of his naked limbs wrapped around hers flashed before her eyes. She barely heard his quietly spoken response.

'I wanted you to see Bainsworth. I thought after seeing it you'd agree more easily to coming here to work on the walled garden renovation project.'

Her already overloaded brain creaked and tried to make sense of what he was saying. 'But why would I come to Bainsworth? My job...my life... is at Loughmore.'

Tom looked at her for long moments, those silver eyes capturing her soul. 'You can divide your time between the two estates.'

'Why would I do that?'

He blinked, worked his jaw. 'To spend time with me.'

She wasn't following, and she certainly wasn't ready to deal with the possible implications of what he was saying, so she asked instead, 'Does that mean you're keeping Loughmore?'

'You were right when you said I had a responsibility to look after the entire estate. I was planning to sell it for the wrong reasons. I was planning to sell it because Loughmore held too many painful memories.'

She winced at his words. 'I think I should resign.'

She craned her neck as he came to stand in front of her again. She hadn't seen him wear this suit and shirt before. For some reason that thought made her feel ridiculously sad. There was so much about his life she had no knowledge of.

His hand reached forward, his fingers lightly, tenderly touching the lapel of her suit. His eyes swallowed her up with gentle certainty. 'I missed you.'

Why was he saying these things to her? It was going to mess up their already uneasy understanding that they would only be friends.

'Did you hear what I said?' she asked.

'You're not resigning. And you're not pushing me away again. I'm here to stay in your life.'

'Please, what's the point? I'm a gardener… you're a duke. We have no future.'

Perching himself on the back of a nearby sofa, Tom reached and pulled her between his parted legs. 'Who we *are* doesn't matter. What matters is that I want to be with you.' He gave her a tentative smile. 'I'm hoping that you want to be with me too.'

She tried to pull away, but his arms on her waist held firm. She placed a hand on his chest, tried to lever herself away. 'But what's the point? You should be thinking about marrying. You need someone with the right background—someone who knows how to be a duchess.'

'I want to be with *you*.'

'For how long, though? I'm a working-class girl from Dublin. We both know I'd be a liability.'

He shook his head, a small smile drifting onto his lips. 'You're wrong, you know. The estate needs a duchess who is smart and intelligent, who can lead the people who work for us. I've seen how you interact with the staff at Loughmore— they love you. You're warm and open…fun to be around. I need a duchess who *gets* me, who supports and believes in me. Someone I can rely on—someone I know will stick by me through life's up and downs.'

He paused, and the certainty in his eyes, that faint smile, disappeared.

He swallowed hard before he asked in a bare whisper, 'Are *you* that person, Ciara?'

It sounded like an ultimatum from Tom, but in truth it wasn't. He was reaching out. Trying to engage her. And it terrified her.

'I don't know.'

Tom blinked. The weight of his hands on her waist lightened momentarily, but then he pulled her even closer, the powerful muscles of his inner thighs pressing against her legs. 'I love you, Ciara. But do you love *me*?'

Stunned, she looked away from his gaze, unable to handle the blazing intensity in his eyes. He'd said he loved her. But he didn't mean it—not really. They were from different worlds, with no future together, and one day soon he'd realise that and walk away. Just as he had done twelve years ago, when he had walked away on that London street. Just as her father had done, leaving behind only a handful of photos that showed him holding her in his arms, beaming proudly into the camera. The picture of a contented dad.

Time and the reality of life destroyed even the strongest love.

She swallowed hard, attempted a laugh. 'You don't mean that. We've been caught up in memories and…and lust.'

'Ciara…'

She winced at the sadness in his voice. And then his hand was on her chin, forcing her to look at him.

He breathed in deeply, as though fortifying himself. 'You have my heart, my soul, my every waking thought. I love you—of that be in no doubt. The question is, again, do you love *me*?'

She looked into the eyes of the one person who made her feel complete, at ease. Who thrilled her. Who filled her life with happiness and hope and dreams. And she answered truthfully, 'I'm scared.'

His forehead dropped gently against hers. Her heart went into freefall. His warmth, his scent, the chemistry playing between them was almost undoing her.

'I'm scared too, but losing you scares me even more,' he said gently. He shifted his head, whispered against her ear, 'Tell me why you're scared. Let me help you.'

Held in his embrace, hearing his softly spoken words, she desperately wanted to pull away. But, as if sensing what she was thinking, Tom curled his hand lightly around the base of her neck, where her hair was pulled up into a high ponytail, his fingers stroking her soothingly, as though trying to ease her panic.

And it worked. In the cocoon of his embrace, his touch, in knowing that he loved her, she felt her panic lessen and found the solace and strength and courage to admit for the first time what was truly in her heart.

'I'm scared that some day you'll realise I'm not what you want, what you need in life. You've apologised a hundred times for how you reacted in London, when I told you I was pregnant, but deep down I still worry that is how you truly feel. That you will reject me like your father rejected my mum.' She pulled back, stared him in the eyes, forcing her words out from a throat that felt narrow and raw. 'I'm scared of losing another baby. I'm scared of losing you again, Tom. I couldn't bear it.'

His thumb rubbed against her cheek, which

was burning hot with the emotion of her admissions. 'So it's easier not to fall in love with me?'

'Yes.'

Tom understood only too well how scared Ciara was feeling. For the past week he had battled his own fears, questioning the wisdom of the path he was taking, waking in the middle of the night racked with doubt. He knew he was running a huge risk, opening up to Ciara about his feelings for her. It would without doubt bring an end to their attempt to be friends and, worse still, it meant he was putting his heart on the line and opening himself up to the potential humiliation and pain of hearing her say she did not love him back.

But in the emptiness of his life without Ciara he had come to realise he needed to find the courage inside himself to reach out to her and fight for their relationship. By their own admission they did not wear their hearts on their sleeves, but that had to change.

'I love you, Ciara. Even though I tried to pretend I had moved on from you when we split, I never stopped loving you. The first time I realised I loved you was that day when we went swimming in the lake—do you remember I hid under the jetty and you called and called for me? When I came out you were crying. No one had ever cared so much for me.'

Her eyes grew wild and angry in remembrance. 'I wanted to kill you.'

He grimaced, held his right bicep. 'I reckon I'm still bruised from where you hit me.'

'You *so* deserved it.'

He could not help but grin at the passionate anger glittering in her eyes. 'Do you believe me when I say that I love you?'

'I'm trying to.'

'It tore me apart when we split. I was ashamed of how badly I reacted when you told me you were pregnant.' A tightness gripped his throat. 'On my flight to Ireland I had worked out a plan for how we would manage. I would move to Dublin to be with you, work double shifts to support you through university while you were pregnant. Once our baby was born I reckoned I could work evening shifts, so that I could mind him during the day…' He swallowed against the ache gripping his throat. 'On the flight back everything was a void. I felt so empty. I had no future.'

Tears shone in Ciara's eyes. He felt tears well

at the back of his eyes too. Pretending everything was okay was so ingrained in him that he struggled to continue, but knew their relationship needed this blunt honesty—no matter how difficult it was to open up, to effectively hand his heart on a platter to Ciara.

'What I feel for you now is even more intense than my love for you before. Being with you over Christmas reminded me of what we had, but I've also fallen in love with the woman you've become—a smart, savvy professional, who's loyal to those she loves. And people love you back. And are loyal to *you*. That's what I need in a duchess most of all—a leader who's respected and loved, who creates loyalty. You'd make a perfect duchess.'

Ciara rolled her eyes. 'A gardener with a tattoo? Hardly. As for being smart—if I was smart I wouldn't be in love with *you*, would I?'

Really? Was *this* the way she was going to tell him?

His heart gave a funny little kick. A broad beam popped onto his face. 'You love me?'

Ciara stepped away, folded her arms and considered him unhappily. 'I'm warning you, Tom, you'd have a much easier future with someone else.'

She loved him! He wanted to take her into his arms, hold her. But this conversation wasn't over yet. Not by a long shot. They had things that needed to be cleared up.

'You said last week that it was my decision as to whether I sell Loughmore or not. You trusted me on that. It means everything to me that you gave me that trust. I thought after my reaction to your pregnancy you'd never trust me again, but you *did*. It gave me hope that you loved me as much as I love you. But why won't you trust me now, in deciding who I want to marry, who I want to spend my life with? I want to have children with you, Ciara. I want to share my life with you.'

'People will talk…disapprove…think you're cracked.'

'And together we'll prove them all wrong.'

She gripped her folded arms even tighter, her eyes clouding with worry. In a quiet voice she asked, 'What if I miscarry again?'

His heart crumbled as he saw her distress. He took her into his arms. Held her. Planted a kiss against her forehead. 'We'll deal with that too.'

'Your family won't approve.'

'Well, we're even on that—nor will yours. Life will have its up and downs, Ciara. I'm not promising you a fairy tale, but we'll be a team. We'll face whatever life throws at us. But the one thing that will kill us as a couple is if we aren't honest with one another—open about what's upsetting us.'

Tom was right. Not being honest, not trusting each other, being too scared to look for support, was what had driven them apart before.

She squeezed her eyes shut, dragged in a breath and, stepping back, admitted, 'I'm terrified you'll walk away from me like my dad did—like your dad walked away from my mum. I'm terrified I'm not what you need...that all we have is this stupid chemistry between us and memories.'

Tom shook his head, his silver gaze never leaving her. 'I promise I will never leave you. How could I when you are the centre of my life? You give me meaning, hope. And as for what I need in my life—well, I reckon what I need more than anything is a feisty redhead who is insightful and empathetic. Who supports me like no one else. Who makes me laugh. Who *gets* me. No one gets me like you do, Ciara. With you I feel complete. I feel alive. Yes, I'm attracted to you to the point of madness—but it's more than that. With you I'm at ease... I'm my true self. Not the Duke of Bainsworth, with all the responsibilities and traditions that go with that. I'm Tom—pure and simple. A man in love with the most incredible woman in this world.'

Ciara could not help but blush—at Tom's words, and even more at the tender love and affection shining in his eyes.

'I got on with my life when we were apart, and I'm proud of how I survived, but there was this emptiness inside me,' she said. 'I tried to ignore how much I missed you, but on your birthday, at Christmas, on Valentine's Day...frankly every day of the year... I thought about you. I felt so *proud* of everything you were achieving.'

Her chest felt as if it was going to explode with the hurt and sadness of all those years.

'But I had lost my soul mate—the person who teased me, who held me when I was down, who told me things would work out. The person who listened to my dreams and didn't dismiss them. And I could do nothing to make that right.'

Tom held out his hand to her, and when she took hold of it he pulled her towards him. Undoing the single button of her suit jacket, he wrapped his arms around her waist, the heavy warmth of his forearms melting through the light cotton of her blouse.

'We've found each other again—let's not waste any more time.'

His hands on her back stroked against her spine. She edged into him.

In a husky voice that matched the dark passion in his eyes, he whispered, 'I want to be with you—today and every day for the rest of our lives.'

A shudder of hope, tenderness and desire ran down the length of her body. 'Sean is expecting me back to work tomorrow.'

'You and I are flying to Dublin tonight on my plane. I need to start work on all those plans you have suggested for making Loughmore financially viable.'

She nodded, but in truth she was still confused. Tentatively she asked, 'So…how do you want to play this? Will we date? See how things work out?'

Tom reared back, stared at her as though she'd just suggested they commit the crime of the century. 'Are you kidding me? After so many years apart, we're not wasting any more time, Ciara Harris!'

Bemused, Ciara watched him walk to his desk, take something from a drawer. Her heart went into orbit when he knelt before her, opening the green velvet box in his hands to reveal an exquisite emerald ring.

'Ciara Harris, will you do me the honour of marrying me?'

Ciara could not help but giggle at the formality of his words, but she soon sobered when she saw the tension in his expression. 'Isn't this all happening a bit too fast?'

'Will you feel any different about me in six months? A year's time?'

He had a point. 'No, I'll still love you to bits.'

'Then why wait?'

She couldn't make this too easy for him. She needed to see him sweat—if only a little bit. 'Only if you promise to come to dance lessons with me before the wedding.'

Still kneeling on the floor, Tom shook his head. 'Now, *that's* a deal-breaker if ever I heard one.'

Ciara laughed, loving the playful mischievous swirling around them, the loving teasing between them, the life-affirming freedom of knowing the person she loved loved her back with the same passion and intensity.

'I love you, Tom Benson. Yes, of course I will marry you.'

His eyes alive with love, Tom placed the ring on her finger, stood, lowered his mouth to hers and whispered, 'And I love *you*, Ciara Harris,' before his mouth caressed her lips with a kiss full of tenderness and dreams and hopes and promises.

# EPILOGUE

THE FOLLOWING CHRISTMAS snow did not arrive at Loughmore. Instead a bright sun gently warmed the land in the days leading up to Christmas Day.

It was on such a gentle day of pale blue skies that Ciara travelled towards the church in Loughmore Village in a horse-drawn carriage, with her grandad on one side, Libby on the other. From the moment they had boarded the carriage, outside the castle, her grandad had held her hand, pride gleaming in his eyes.

At first when they had announced their engagement both families had been alarmed, but for the past year she and Tom had worked hard to include them all in the wedding plans. And as the months had passed by, and both families had seen close at hand not only their love and support for one another, but the way they wanted to become part of their new extended families, they had come round to accepting their marriage.

Sitting on the opposite bench, her flower girls

giggled as the carriage hit the brow of a steep hill and the four horses began to canter down the opposite side. Grace Carney, Sophie O'Brien and Grace McCarthy all looked angelic in their floor-length white tulle skirts and white fake fur jackets with matching mufflers.

Fiddling with the ivy wreath in her hair, Grace Carney stopped giggling and fixed a look of deep concentration on Ciara. 'If you and the Prince have a baby will she be a princess?'

Ciara bit back a smile, remembering Tom's whispered words last week, before she had left Bainsworth to return to Loughmore to prepare for the wedding, about how they were going to spend their entire honeymoon on the Bensons' private St Lucia resort making babies.

A week away from him had been torture. For the past year they had rarely spent any time apart. Tom had worked mostly from his offices at Bainsworth and Loughmore, between which they were now dividing their time.

She edged towards the girls—not an easy feat with the weight of her full-skirted lace dress and its long train. She had fallen in love with it in a Paris showroom, and Danny and Libby, her wedding-dress-buying companions, had both cried when she'd stepped out of the dressing room and insisted she buy it immediately.

Now she answered Grace's question. 'Not a princess but a *lady*.'

All three girls were rosy-cheeked from the cold, but shy Grace blushed even more as she asked hesitantly, 'Ciara, will…will you dance with me at the party?'

Ciara's heart swelled at Grace's shyness and she blinked back fresh tears. Was she *really* about to marry Tom Benson, the love of her life, surrounded by all the people she loved in this world? Not for the first time she wanted to pinch herself to see if this was really happening to her.

'Of course I'll dance with you, Grace.'

Beside her, Libby grumbled. 'God, I'm not sure I'll be able to dance in this dress—it's digging into my ribs.'

Ciara eyed Libby and laughed. They both knew Libby's full-length champagne tulle dress with matching fake fur jacket fitted her perfectly. She was only complaining because of her nervousness—something Ciara had been teasing her about all morning, pointing out it was *she* who should be nervous, not Libby.

And that was the curious thing. She wasn't nervous. Instead she felt a calmness. A peace of mind and a joy that she was about to marry the man who loved her so deeply.

Every day for the past year he had shown his love to her. Often in small ways. A phone call when she needed it. Whisking her away for walks in the woods when she was stressed with the work of helping transform some areas of Loughmore into visitor centres alongside the newly appointed Loughmore Events Manager and her team.

He had also insisted that they spend a week with her grandparents in their home in Renvyle. It had been a week full of love and laughter, of early-morning swims in the Atlantic and sunset horse-rides on the deserted beaches of Connemara.

And he had invited her mum to cut the ribbon on the opening night of Tom's, Loughmore. She had performed with her usual 'not-fussed' demeanour, but deep down Ciara had seen her mum's delight at appearing in all the national newspapers standing alongside her famous soon-to-be son-in-law.

And then there had been his insistence that their wedding guest list wouldn't just involve the usual dignitaries, but also all their friends and the staff.

Libby's glossy chestnut hair was hanging loose, just as Ciara's was, and Libby was wearing a tiara made of a single strand of diamonds. Ciara was wearing the Benson family diamond and platinum halo tiara and a long veil.

Ciara took Libby's hand. 'You look gorgeous—and I bet Evan will agree.'

Libby shrugged, trying very hard not to look delighted. Ciara held her hand even tighter, feeling how it was trembling. Libby and Evan had been dating for over two months now. Evan had transferred from Tom's, Cambridge, to head up the new Loughmore restaurant, and both chefs had instantly hit it off.

A few weeks into their relationship Tom had finally admitted to Ciara that he had asked Evan to transfer to Loughmore because he'd had an instinct Evan and Libby would make an ideal couple.

There were crowds lining the streets of Loughmore, and when the carriage came into view applause rang out. Some called to her grandad, who was now beaming from ear to ear, others called to the flower girls, who were waving wildly to all they knew.

Ciara's calmness deserted her, to be replaced by rampant butterflies in her stomach.

Outside the church her mum fussed around her, fixing her dress as newspaper photographers snapped away.

Then her mum gave her a quick hug and whispered into her ear, 'You look deadly, pet—the absolute bee's knees. Now, be a good girl and try not to make a holy show of yourself by tripping in the aisle.'

She disappeared into the church.

His eyes fixed on the stained-glass window towering over the altar, focused on breathing in deeply and exhaling slowly, trying not to allow his leg to jig up and down, Tom heard laughter moving down the aisle.

Ciara! She was here!

From the corner of his eye he spotted her mum taking her seat on the opposite side of the aisle. At first wary of him, Ciara's mum Bernie had slowly softened towards him over the past year. A large lump had formed in his throat earlier, when she had fussed over his lopsided buttonhole. Repinning it, she had called him a 'big eejit' before giving him a quick hug and scuttling off to talk to his mother. Much to his surprise, his mother had instantly taken to Bernie, explaining that she enjoyed Bernie's frankness and wicked sense of humour.

'Maybe she's having second thoughts?'

He eyed Fran, who was seated behind him and had sat forward to tease him with an evil look in her eye.

Kitty decided to join in too. 'We told her to run at the hen party, but she wouldn't listen.'

His sisters had initially been cautious around Ciara, intent on protecting their big brother and more than a little put out that their matchmaking hopes for linking him up with one of their friends were over. But over the Easter weekend, which they all spent at Bainsworth Hall, they had got to know Ciara's irreverent humour and loveliness and quickly decided to be on 'Team Ciara'.

The minister stepped out in front of the altar. Beamed down towards the end of the church.

Charlie Perry, an old schoolfriend of his who was now a guitarist in a world-famous band, began to play Pachelbel's 'Canon in D,' the soulful notes rising up to the vaulted roof of the church.

Tom stood, blinking back tears. He had lost her for too long. He had lost the person he was. But now life was once again full of colour and possibilities and love.

He turned. His heart somersaulted. Beyond the giggling flower girls and a blushing Libby the love of his life was walking towards him, with Charlie's tender rendition of the music guiding her every step.

Fresh tears flooded his eyes. He wiped them away, not caring that all the guests would see. He loved this beautiful, strong and intelligent woman whose heart was spun from gold.

When she finally came to stand beside him he hugged her grandfather and then turned to her. They were both crying. They both knew what it was to lose one another. And how precious, how miraculous it was to find one another again.

He pulled her into him, felt their tears mingling. He whispered, 'I'll love you for a thousand years and more.'

She pulled away, sniffed, laughed. She held his hand and smiled, her eyes blazing with love. 'I've

dreamt about this moment for years and years…
I never thought it would actually happen.'

He touched his thumb against her cheek, wiping the tears away. 'Ready?'

She nodded. And together they turned to the minister knowing friendship and hope and above all love would bond them together for ever.

\* \* \* \* \*

# LET'S TALK
## Romance

For exclusive extracts, competitions and special offers, find us online:

f facebook.com/millsandboon

⊙ @millsandboonuk

🐦 @millsandboon

Or get in touch on 0844 844 1351*

For all the latest titles coming soon,
visit millsandboon.co.uk/nextmonth

*Calls cost 7p per minute plus your phone company's price per minute access charge